Robert Louis Stevenson (1850–94) was born in Edinburgh. In the brief span of forty-four years, dogged by poor health, he made an enormous contribution to English literature with his novels, poetry, and essays. The son of upper-middle-class parents, he was the victim of lung trouble from birth and spent a sheltered childhood surrounded by constant care. In 1880, he married Mrs. Fanny Osbourne, a woman ten years his senior. The balance of his life was taken up with his unremitting devotion to work and a search for a cure to his illness that took him all over the world. His travel essays were published widely, and his short fiction was gathered in many volumes. His first full-length work of fiction, *Treasure Island*, was published in 1883 and brought him great fame, which only increased with the publication of *The Strange Case of Dr. Jekyll and Mr. Hyde* (1886). He followed with the Scottish romances *Kidnapped* (1886) and *The Master of Ballantrae* (1889). In 1888, he set out with his family for the South Seas, traveling to the leper colony at Molokai, and finally settling in Samoa, where he died.

Kelly Hurley is an Associate Professor of English at the University of Colorado at Boulder, where she teaches Victorian studies, literary theory, and popular culture. She is the author of *The Gothic Body: Sexuality, Materialism, and Degeneration at the Fin de Siècle*, as well as various articles on Victorian and contemporary Gothic. Her next book is on horror film spectatorship.

continued . . .

Vladimir Nabokov (1899–1977) was born in St. Petersburg, Russia, in a trilingual household; he could read and write in English before Russian or French. His family went into exile after the Bolshevik revolution and lived in various European cities, including Berlin and Prague. In 1940, Nabokov and his wife and son fled from the Nazis to America, where he taught college and wrote *Lolita* (1955). After that book's tremendous success, he was able to write full-time and moved back to Europe, eventually settling in Montreaux, Switzerland. Among his other notable books are *Pale Fire* (1962) and *Ada* (1969). In addition to his writing, he was a noted entomologist specializing in butterflies.

Dan Chaon is the author of the novels *Await Your Reply* and *You Remind Me of Me*, and two short story collections, *Fitting Ends* and the 2001 National Book Award Finalist *Among the Missing*. His work has appeared in numerous magazines, including *Story*, *Ploughshares*, and *TriQuarterly*, as well as *Best American Short Stories* and *The Pushcart Prize 2000*. The recipient of numerous prizes and honors, he is the Pauline Delaney Professor of Creative Writing and Literature at Oberlin College.

DR. JEKYLL
AND MR. HYDE

―――⚬⚬⚬―――

Robert Louis Stevenson

With an Introduction by
Kelly Hurley
and an Introductory Essay by
Vladimir Nabokov
and an Afterword by
Dan Chaon

SIGNET CLASSICS
New York

SIGNET CLASSICS
Published by Berkley
An imprint of Penguin Random House LLC
penguinrandomhouse.com

Introduction copyright © 2012 by Kelly Hurley
"The Strange Case of Dr. Jekyll and Mr. Hyde" copyright © 1980 by
The Estate of Vladimir Nabokov. Reprinted by permission of Harcourt, Inc.
Afterword copyright © 2003 by Dan Chaon

ISBN: 9780593438510

First Signet Classics mass-market edition / October 1987
First Signet Classics mass-market edition (Hurley introduction) / December 2012
First Signet Classics trade edition / August 2021

Printed in the United States of America
1st Printing

CONTENTS

INTRODUCTION
IN DREAMS

Discussions of *Dr. Jekyll and Mr. Hyde* often begin with the story of a dream, Robert Louis Stevenson's dream, recounted in a 1901 biography by his cousin Graham Balfour. Fanny Stevenson was awakened one night by her sleeping husband's "cries of horror" and hastened to rouse him from his nightmare. Rather than thanking his wife, however, he reproached her furiously. "Why did you wake me? I was dreaming a fine bogey tale." This nightmare of a "bogey" or monster became the core of the short novel that would be written and rewritten "at a red heat" by an author transfixed by his own dream, and composing as if "in a fever." In a magazine essay published two years later, Stevenson credited the dream with having provided "the central idea of a voluntary change becoming involuntary," the plot device of the powder by which the transformation is initially effected, and three specific "scenes" that would be incorporated into the novel.

One of these scenes is found in the chapter entitled "Incident at the Window" (page 85–86). Mr. Utterson, Dr. Jekyll's lawyer and good friend, is out for his usual Sunday

7

walk with his cousin Mr. Enfield when they find Jekyll sitting at a window above the courtyard of his house "like some disconsolate prisoner." Jekyll, who has mysteriously isolated himself for some weeks, will not come down to join them or invite them up, instead asking them, almost pathetically, to linger outside and keep him company. "But the words were hardly uttered, before the smile was struck out of his face and succeeded by an expression of such abject terror and despair, as froze the very blood of the two gentlemen below." The voluntary change has become involuntary, or at least we know this in retrospect. Jekyll slams down the window before the two men can observe his uncontrollable metamorphosis into Mr. Hyde. Utterson and Enfield stand in stunned silence, "an answering horror in their eyes."

The scene is remarkably unsettling, and this is all the more remarkable given that so little is actually shown. It is like a dream sequence whose haunting effect exceeds the sum of its parts. Utterson and Enfield have no idea what terrible thing is happening behind the window, and the first-time reader, too, can only speculate uneasily as to what this might be. But the scene does not lose its power upon further readings. The window slamming shut just before the change can be witnessed. The body that turns against itself. The identity that churns and dissolves and comes together again in an unspeakable form. The "answering horror" that passes from Jekyll to the two onlookers to the reader like a contagion. The traumatic event that is represented and that is not represented.

Utterson and Enfield exit the courtyard "without a word." This refusal—or inability—to speak of what is happening is not untypical in the novel, and enhances its dreamlike quality. Hyde is himself like a figure from a dream: he inspires a "haunting sense" of uneasiness, a sense of *wrongness*, that no one can explain or understand (page 73). Enfield admits, "I never saw a man I so disliked, and yet I scarce know why" (page 53). There is "something abnormal and misbegotten in the very essence" of Hyde, says Lanyon, "something seizing, surprising, and revolting" (page 106). Hyde's is "the fascination of the abomination," to quote Joseph Conrad's *Heart of Darkness* (1899). He arouses in Lanyon "a disgustful curiosity," in Utterson a "hitherto unknown disgust, loathing and fear" (pages 106, 61).

And yet Utterson cannot stop thinking about Hyde. He is no less disturbed by his good friend's "strange preference or bondage" to the man than by Hyde's callous acts of brutality on the London streets (page 58). Utterson's "imagination" becomes "engaged, or rather enslaved," by Hyde and by the mystery of Hyde's relationship to Jekyll. Thus imaginatively enslaved, Utterson is "haunted" by a dream of his own, in which two sequences are repeated. In one, he sees the terrible figure of Hyde moving "the more swiftly and still the more swiftly" through the "labyrinths of [the] lamp-lighted city," so that "at every street corner" he would "crush a child and leave her screaming." In the other, this figure steals to the bedroom of the sleeping Jekyll and pulls his bed curtains apart and orders him to "rise and do its bidding."

What lies behind, or beneath, the uncanny figure of Hyde that enables it to enslave the imagination? Readers and critics have struggled with this question since the novel was published. Hyde commits two acts of shocking violence, but they cannot quite account for his loathsome *suchness*. In an 1886 letter Gerard Manley Hopkins wrote, "The trampling scene is perhaps a convention: [Stevenson] was thinking of something unsuitable for fiction." But beyond the trampling and the murder, as Vladimir Nabokov complains, we are favored with "unspecified, vague, but ominous allusions to pleasures and dreadful vices" (page 31).

"[T]his is a private matter, and I beg of you to let it sleep." Thus Jekyll reproaches Utterson, who reluctantly gives his promise (page 67). At times the characters' silences and acts of silencing seem like part of a tacit gentlemen's agreement to overlook one another's immoral or illegal acts and protect one another's good reputation. "I make it a rule of mine" not to ask questions about other men's indiscretions, says Enfield, the "man about town" who himself can be found roaming the London streets at three in the morning. "A very good rule, too," replies Utterson, for straitlaced and "austere" as he is, Utterson has "an approved tolerance" for gentlemanly "misdeeds," and is "inclined to help rather than to reprove" the sinner (pages 52, 47).

Utterson fears that Hyde is blackmailing Jekyll for some long-forgotten "sin" or "disgrace," for he knows that Jekyll "was wild when he was young" (page 63). Perhaps Utterson suspects that Jekyll has engaged in acts of heterosexual profligacy—visiting prostitutes, corrupting young ladies, seducing respectable married women—in violation of the Victorian norms of gentlemanly honor and restraint. Perhaps Hyde is Jekyll's illegitimate son. Or perhaps Hyde is Jekyll's lover—a possibility that Elaine Showalter argues is obliquely suggested within the novel in scenes like the dream of Hyde coming to Jekyll's bedside. Both socially tabooed and illegal, homosexuality was "unspeakable" in a certain sense in the late nineteenth century: "the love that dare not speak its name." The 1885 Labouchère Amendment, which prohibited acts of "gross indecency" and was used to prosecute male homosexuals, was popularly known as the "blackmailer's charter."

Since Jekyll *is* Hyde, of course, none of these possibilities can be correct. But *Jekyll and Hyde* entertains them, and this allows us to attend to some of the controversies and concerns that were widespread within late-Victorian Britain, and emerge to trouble the novel. The Gothic is sometimes understood as a genre that negotiates anxieties for its host culture by working through them in displaced fashion, particularly by means of its monsters. And as the critics have shown, even the stunted figure of Hyde turns out to be capacious enough to embody any number of cultural anxieties—about sexuality, about urban modernity, about new scientific theories of human identity. With his coarse incivility and eruptive violence, Hyde may be said to give form to Victorian fears of an insurgent urban working class. Hyde is also an "animal," a "thing like a monkey" (pages 96, 94). He is the Gothic's answer to the concluding sentence of Charles Darwin's 1871 *The Descent of Man*: "Man still bears in his bodily frame the indelible stamp of his lowly origin." The composite being Jekyll/Hyde might suggest for the Victorian reader the possibility that the evolution of human beings is a very partial and incomplete process, for Hyde is an "ape-like" primitive, and Jekyll can no longer control his own reversion into this primitive type (page 69).

When Stevenson's novel was first published, its full title was *Strange Case of Dr. Jekyll and Mr. Hyde*. The title is often abbreviated to emphasize the doubling relationship that stands as the heart of the novel. But it is worth thinking about why Stevenson chose to present this relationship as a "strange case." The *Oxford English Dictionary* tells us that some of the older, basic meanings of the word *case* include "the actual state or position of matters," or "a thing that befalls or happens to any one." Thus *strange case* could simply allude to the unusual circumstances within which the hapless Jekyll becomes entangled.

But *case* accrued new, more technical meanings in the nineteenth century, and I want to consider Stevenson's title in relation to some of these. One of them is "an incident or set of circumstances requiring investigation by the police or other detective agency"—an important meaning in the century that saw the formal establishment of a standing police force in Great Britain. Jekyll/Hyde's is not exactly a police case, nor is it a legal case. The police solve the murder of Sir Danvers Carew almost immediately (Hyde is easily proved to be the killer) but cannot bring the case to a close after Hyde's seeming disappearance. Enfield and the doctor who attends the trampled child do not even call the police, but decide to privately extort Hyde on behalf of the little girl's family. "No gentleman but wishes to avoid a scene" (page 51). Utterson, anxious to preserve the reputation of his old friend for as long as possible, hides information from the police—for example, the fact that the walking stick with which Hyde murdered Carew was a gift that Utterson "had himself presented many years before to Henry Jekyll" (page 70). And after Hyde's suicide Utterson refuses to notify the police until he has had a chance to read Lanyon's and Jekyll's explanatory documents. The novel then ends abruptly after Jekyll's "Full Statement of the Case." Presumably the police eventually arrived to collect the guilty Hyde's corpse, but the novel does not bother to represent this, and we can also presume that Utterson kept back the "full statement" that would have implicated Dr. Jekyll in Mr. Hyde's crimes.

Utterson's gentlemanly preoccupation with privacy could remind us of the private detective, also a creation of the nineteenth century. The private investigator provided an alternative for clients who wished to solve a crime or mystery but avoid the public scrutiny and bureaucratic entanglements that might result from an official consultation with the police. This in turn could remind us of that increasingly popular new literary genre, detective fiction, associated with such figures as Edgar Allan Poe, Wilkie Collins, and Émile Gaboriau, the American, English, and French authors who featured amateur or consulting detectives in works like "The Murders in the Rue Morgue" (1841), *The Woman in White* (1859–60), and *L'Affaire Lerouge* (1865). Dan Chaon describes *Jekyll and Hyde* as a kind of detective story, at least structurally. "With its obliquely recorded incidents, its eyewitness accounts and sealed confessions, it resembles nothing so much as a casebook—a collection of gathered clues, fragments, through which the clever detective may be able to intuit or project a complete narrative" (page 135). Clearly *case* was available to Stevenson in this context as well, especially if we imagine Utterson as a reluctant amateur detective determined to solve the mystery of the strange relationship between Jekyll and Hyde and unmask the criminal who seems to threaten his old friend. The word had been used in the title of a detective novel just a few years earlier, Anna Katharine Green's *The Leavenworth Case* (1878).

Similar titles (Arthur Morrison's "The Case of the Dixon Torpedo," Sir Arthur Conan Doyle's Sherlock Holmes story "A Case of Identity") would become fairly common in detective fiction of the 1890s and afterward, but were rare in the years before *Jekyll and Hyde* was published. Perhaps it is more fruitful to consider another type of usage available when Stevenson was writing his "Strange Case." The medical meaning of *case* as "the condition" or "record of the progress of disease in an individual" goes back at least to the early 1700s, according to the *OED*. The word would become increasingly important in nineteenth-century social medicine: in new disciplines like sexology, criminology, and psychiatry, which took as their special province the study of human pathology. The "deviant" subject (so-called) was a *case*, often a numbered case in the casebook of the scientific professional. The scientific write-up of the deviant was also a *case*, or a case study, a quasi-narrative document that tracked the inception, development, and behavioral and physical manifestations of the pathology in question, whether that might be sexual sadism, an innate predisposition to crime, or mental aberration. For example, in 1836 the psychologist Robert Macnish described the "case" of a "young lady" who lost her memory and had to start over and acquire a new set of experiences and memories. She then suddenly recalled her original identity and henceforth alternated between the old and new personalities. In 1860 this would be written up for *Harper's New Monthly Magazine* as "Mary Reynolds: A Case of Double Consciousness."

If Jekyll/Hyde can be read as a sociomedical *case*, what kind of case is he? "I thus drew steadily nearer to that truth," writes Dr. Jekyll, "that man is not truly one, but truly two. . . . [O]thers will outstrip me on the same lines; and I hazard the guess that man will be ultimately known for a mere polity of multifarious, incongruous and independent denizens" (page 111). The late-nineteenth-century human sciences entertained a number of theories of a divided self, split into two or perhaps more chaotically disunified. One prominent theory of homosexuality, for example, understood it a kind of doubled identity known as "sexual inversion." The male homosexual was "a female soul united with a male body." His masculine body was self-contradicted by his feminine attributes, predilections, and desires. (The male invert's opposite number, to quote from Richard von Krafft-Ebing's 1886 *Psychopathia Sexualis*, suffered from a "masculine soul heaving in the female bosom.") Criminology borrowed from evolutionary biology to describe another pathologically divided subject: the "atavist," an evolutionary throwback whose innate propensity for criminality could be explained by his body's reactivation of primitive traits that were dormant in the ordinary subject. The atavist was a "born criminal" innately prone to reversion, his human identity shot through with a brutal animalism.

Victorian psychology especially explored the divisions within the human subject. These might be pathological, like the extreme dissociation or "double consciousness" experienced by Mary Reynolds. Another such category was "moral insanity," described by James Cowles Prichard in 1835. Moral insanity was a form of *partial* insanity that left "the reasoning faculties" intact, but caused "a morbid perversion of the natural feelings, affections, inclinations, temper," and moral character. Sufferers manifested Jekyll-and-Hyde-like oscillations of behavior; normally decorous, they would suddenly lose the "power of self-government" and behave in ways that were "strangely perverted and depraved."

More disturbingly, self-division might characterize *all* human subjects, not just pathological ones. Victorian psychologists described a psyche unknown to itself, concealed from itself, haunted by itself. They studied unconscious mental processes, instinctive and automatic modes of thought, the human susceptibility to trancelike and dreamlike states. They posited a layered and even discontinuous psychic structure. In an article published a few months after Stevenson's *Strange Case*, Frederick W. H. Myers characterized human identity as "multiplex and mutable," susceptible to ceaseless change and to "morbid disintegration." Our very "being," he suggested, is no more than a "shifting sand-heap." Dr. Jekyll writes of how his experiments caused the "fortress of identity" to be shaken and breached (page 113). But the psychic structure as described within Victorian psychology was never a fortress, nor even a unified structure at all.

As I conclude I wish to turn to perhaps the most famous writer on the "strange case" of the divided, tumultuous human psyche. Sigmund Freud and Stevenson were near contemporaries, born six years apart, although Stevenson did not survive the nineteenth century and Freud lived far into the twentieth. Freud published his *Interpretation of Dreams* only fourteen years after the debut of *Jekyll and Hyde*. His emphasis, as the title indicates, is on interpretation—the interpretation of those absurdist documents known as dreams, so disjointed and incomprehensible, often so horrifying. Freud's study provides methods of reading useful to literary analysis, especially the analysis of the nightmarish Gothic, with its distorted human figures, its gloomy settings, its narrative disjunctions, its unsettling tone. Literary texts are not dreams, of course, and are constructed by different processes than dreams. Stevenson labored over several drafts of the novel, elaborating and recasting the material of his originary dream quite extensively. But its dreamlike quality remains, and retains the ability to disturb even after we have considered the "strange case" from every possible angle. "There must be something else," as Utterson says of Hyde. "There *is* something more, if I could find a name for it" (page 61).

In his analysis of dreams, Freud distinguishes between *manifest content* and *latent content*: between the images and narrative sequences set out in a dream, and the fears, desires, and anxieties that underlie them. "The dream-thoughts and the dream-content," that is, the latent and manifest content, "are presented to us like two versions of the same subject-matter in two different languages. Or, more properly, the dream-content seems like a transcript of the dream-thoughts into another mode of expression, whose characters and syntactic laws it is our business to discover by comparing the original and the translation."

This comparison, however, is by no means a simple or straightforward process. In the first place, according to Freud, the latent content of the dream is often inaccessible, consisting of ideas or emotions that the conscious self finds unacceptable or intolerable and thus represses, banishing them to the unconscious. In an ongoing and dynamic tension, repressed content struggles to become known, and the conscious mind struggles to silence and "forget" what it cannot bear to acknowledge. In dreams, repressed content emerges by means of a *compromise formation*: it finds expression, but only in a transmogrified form, an unrecognizable form, allowing the conscious mind to remain ignorant of what it has repressed.

The *dream-work* labors to maintain this compromise, using a number of methods to distort latent content and render it unrecognizable. Dreams have their own "syntactic laws" designed to confuse the dreamer. They mix up logical sequences (for example, reversing cause and effect) and invert affect, so that a wish may be represented as a fear. They juxtapose seemingly unrelated elements, so that one must interpret in terms of contiguity—the fact that one thing stands next to another or one event occurs right after another. (If a dream depicts a happy family picnic being overrun by zombies, the idea of cannibalistic monstrosity probably has more to do with the family than the zombies.) Dreams admix troublesome latent material with the *residue* of the previous day's ordinary events so that one cannot be sure if a dream-element is meaningful or banal.

Dreams also work through *condensation*: the compression of one, very complex idea or emotion into a brief, evocative image or narrative sequence. To complicate it further, dreams often condense several ideas into the image or sequence, speaking to a variety of traumas simultaneously. Thus the dream is *overdetermined*: it must be read within a number of different, perhaps unrelated contexts. And within the dream each strand of the latent content has been transformed phantasmatically by the dreamwork. Freud writes that the "whole mass" of "dreamthoughts is brought under the pressure of the dream-work, and its elements are turned about, broken into fragments, and jammed together—almost like pack-ice."

Freud intended dream-analysis as a method that would help patients uncover and come to terms with the contents of the unconscious, but with this metaphor Freud tacitly acknowledges that no dream is fully interpretable. The distorting effect of the dream-work is too intense. Put differently, we might say that the unexpectedly creative powers of the dream-work are too much in play—its ability to disguise, combine, superimpose, invert, admix, transfigure the elements of latent content. The dream-work effects an astonishing metamorphosis.

There is no single answer to what Hyde is, to what Hyde means. He is a bewilderingly overdetermined figure. He is an "amorphous" being that "seemed to utter cries and voices," but in no articulate language that we can understand (page 128). In his strange, repulsive body we find the shards of many anxieties that have been broken apart, reshapen, and shoved together, "almost like pack-ice." Polar pack-ice builds up over months or years as a rough sheet that varies in thickness. It melts and refreezes unevenly. It shifts with the wind and ocean currents. Sometimes, it suddenly breaks apart and reveals in its cracks and channels the unfathomable depths of the dark sea.

—Kelly Hurley

Introductory Essay
"The Strange Case of
Dr. Jekyll and Mr. Hyde"*

"Dr. Jekyll and Mr. Hyde" was written in bed, at Bournemouth on the English Channel, in 1885 in between hemorrhages from the lungs. It was published in January 1886. Dr. Jekyll is a fat, benevolent physician, not without human frailties, who at times by means of a potion projects himself into, or concentrates or precipitates, an evil person of brutal and animal nature taking the name of Hyde, in which character he leads a patchy criminal life of sorts. For a time he is able to revert to his Jekyll personality—there is a down-to-Hyde drug and a back-to-Jekyll drug—but gradually his better nature weakens and finally the back-to-Jekyll potion fails, and he poisons himself when on the verge of exposure. This is the bald plot of the story.

First of all, if you have the Pocket Books edition I

*Editor's note: In 1948 Vladimir Nabokov was appointed Associate Professor of Slavic Literature at Cornell University, where he taught Russian Literature in Translation and Masters of European Fiction. For the next ten years he introduced undergraduates to the delights of great fiction, including *Dr. Jekyll and Mr. Hyde,* in fifty-minute classroom lectures. In 1980 his notes were collected by Fredson Bowers and published by Harcourt Brace Jovanovich as *Lectures on Literature,* from which this essay has been reprinted by permission.

have, you will veil the monstrous, abominable, atrocious, criminal, foul, vile, youth-depraving jacket—or better say straitjacket. You will ignore the fact that ham actors under the direction of pork packers have acted in a parody of the book, which parody was then photographed on a film and showed in places called theaters; it seems to me that to call a movie house a theater is the same as to call an undertaker a mortician.

And now comes my main injunction. Please completely forget, disremember, obliterate, unlearn, consign to oblivion any notion you may have had that "Jekyll and Hyde" is some kind of a mystery story, a detective story, or movie. It is of course quite true that Stevenson's short novel, written in 1885, is one of the ancestors of the modern mystery story. But today's mystery story is the very negation of style, being, at the best, conventional literature. Frankly, I am not one of those college professors who coyly boasts of enjoying detective stories—they are too badly written for my taste and bore me to death. Whereas Stevenson's story is—God bless his pure soul—lame as a detective story. Neither is it a parable nor an allegory, for it would be tasteless as either. It has, however, its own special enchantment if we regard it as a phenomenon of style. It is not only a good "bogey story," as Stevenson exclaimed when awakening from a dream in which he had visualized it much in the same way I suppose as magic cerebration had granted Coleridge the vision of the most famous of unfinished poems. It is also, and more importantly, "a fable that lies nearer to poetry than to ordinary prose fiction,"* and therefore belongs to the

---

*Nabokov states that critical quotations in this essay are drawn from Stephen Gwynn, *Robert Louis Stevenson* (London: Macmillan, 1939). Ed.

same order of art as, for instance, *Madame Bovary* or *Dead Souls*.

There is a delightful winey taste about this book; in fact, a good deal of old mellow wine is drunk in the story: one recalls the wine that Utterson so comfortably sips. This sparkling and comforting draft is very different from the icy pangs caused by the chameleon liquor, the magic reagent that Jekyll brews in his dusty laboratory. Everything is very appetizingly put. Gabriel John Utterson of Gaunt Street mouths his words most roundly; there is an appetizing tang about the chill morning in London, and there is even a certain richness of tone in the description of the horrible sensations Jekyll undergoes during his *hydizations*. Stevenson had to rely on style very much in order to perform the trick, in order to master the two main difficulties confronting him: (1) to make the magic potion a plausible drug based on a chemist's ingredients and (2) to make Jekyll's evil side before and after the hydization a believable evil.

[Here Nabokov quoted from "I was so far in my reflections . . ." through "mankind, was pure evil," pp. 10–13.]*

The names Jekyll and Hyde are of Scandinavian origin, and I suspect that Stevenson chose them from the same page of an old book on surnames where I looked them up myself. Hyde comes from the Anglo-Saxon *hyd,* which is the Danish *hide,* "a haven." And Jekyll comes from the Danish name *Jökulle,* which means "an icicle." Not knowing these simple derivations one would be apt to find all kinds of symbolic meanings, especially in

*Editor's note: Throughout his lecture, Nabokov quoted extensively from the novel. For this essay, we provide the beginning and the ending passages that he quoted, with the corresponding page numbers from this edition.

Hyde, the most obvious being that Hyde is a kind of hiding place for Dr. Jekyll, in whom the jocular doctor and the killer are combined.

Three important points are completely obliterated by the popular notions about this seldom read book:

1. Is Jekyll good? No, he is a composite being, a mixture of good and bad, a preparation consisting of a ninety-nine percent solution of Jekyllite and one percent of Hyde (or *hydatid* from the Greek "water" which in zoology is a tiny pouch within the body of man and other animals, a pouch containing a limpid fluid with larval tapeworms in it—a delightful arrangement, for the little tapeworms at least. Thus in a sense, Mr. Hyde is Dr. Jekyll's parasite—but I must warn that Stevenson knew nothing of this when he chose the name). Jekyll's morals are poor from the Victorian point of view. He is a hypocritical creature carefully concealing his little sins. He is vindictive, never forgiving Dr. Lanyon with whom he disagrees in scientific matters. He is foolhardy. Hyde is mingled with him, within him. In this mixture of good and bad in Dr. Jekyll, the bad can be separated as Hyde, who is a precipitate of pure evil, a precipitation in the chemical sense since something of the composite Jekyll remains behind to wonder in horror at Hyde while Hyde is in action.

2. Jekyll is not really transformed into Hyde but projects a concentrate of pure evil that becomes Hyde, who is smaller than Jekyll, a big man, to indicate the larger amount of good that Jekyll possesses.

3. There are really three personalities—Jekyll, Hyde, and a third, the Jekyll residue when Hyde takes over.

The situation may be represented visually.

Henry Jekyll
(large)

Edward Hyde
(small)

But if you look closely you see that within this big, luminous, pleasantly tweed Jekyll there are scattered rudiments of evil.

When the magic drug starts to work, a dark concentration of this evil begins forming

and is projected or ejected as

Still, if you look closely at Hyde, you will notice that above him floats aghast, but dominating, a residue of Jekyll, a kind of smoke ring, or halo, as if this black concentrated evil had fallen out of the remaining ring of good, but this ring of good still remains: Hyde still wants to change back to Jekyll. This is the significant point.

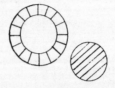

It follows that Jekyll's transformation implies a concentration of evil that already inhabited him rather than a complete metamorphosis. Jekyll is not pure good, and Hyde (Jekyll's statement to the contrary) is not pure evil, for just as parts of unacceptable Hyde dwell within acceptable Jekyll, so over Hyde hovers a halo of Jekyll, horrified at his worser half's iniquity.

The relations of the two are typified by Jekyll's house, which is half Jekyll and half Hyde. As Utterson and his friend Enfield were taking a ramble one Sunday they came to a bystreet in a busy quarter of London which, though small and what is called quiet, drove a thriving trade on weekdays. "Even on Sunday, when it veiled its more florid charms and lay comparatively empty of passage, the street shone out in contrast to its dingy neighbourhood, like a fire in a forest; and with its freshly painted shutters, well-polished brasses, and general cleanliness and gaiety of note, instantly caught and pleased the eye of the passenger.

"Two doors from one corner, on the left hand going east, the line was broken by the entry of a court; and just at that point, a certain sinister block of building thrust forward its gable on the street. It was two storeys high; showed no window, nothing but a door on the lower storey and a blind forehead of discoloured wall on the upper; and bore in every feature, the marks of prolonged and sordid negligence. The door, which was equipped

with neither bell nor knocker, was blistered and dis-
tained. Tramps slouched into the recess and struck
matches on the panels; children kept shop upon the
steps; the schoolboy had tried his knife on the mould-
ings; and for close on a generation, no one had appeared
to drive away these random visitors or repair their ravages."

This is the door that Enfield points out to Utterson
with his cane, which was used by a repugnantly evil man
who had deliberately trampled over a running young girl
and, being collared by Enfield, had agreed to recom-
pense the child's parents with a hundred pounds. Opening the door with a key, he had returned with ten pounds
in gold and a cheque for the remainder signed by Dr.
Jekyll, which proves to be valid. Blackmail, thinks Enfield. He continues to Utterson: "It seems scarcely a
house. There is no other door, and nobody goes in or out
of that one but, once in a great while, the gentleman of
my adventure. There are three windows looking on the
court on the first floor; none below; the windows are always shut but they're clean. And then there is a chimney
which is generally smoking; so somebody must live there.
And yet it's not so sure; for the buildings are so packed
together about that court, that it's hard to say where one
ends and another begins."

Around the corner from the bystreet there is a square
of ancient, handsome houses, somewhat run to seed and
cut up into flats and chambers. "One house, however,
second from the corner, was still occupied entire; and at
the door of this, which wore a great air of wealth and
comfort," Utterson was to knock and inquire for his
friend, Dr. Jekyll. Utterson knows that the door of the
building through which Mr. Hyde had passed is the door
to the old dissecting room of the surgeon who had owned
the house before Dr. Jekyll bought it and that it is a part

of the elegant house fronting on the square. The dissecting room Dr. Jekyll had altered for his chemical experiments, and it was there (we learn much later) that he
made his transformations into Mr. Hyde, at which times
Hyde lived in that wing.

Just as Jekyll is a mixture of good and bad, so Jekyll's
dwelling place is also a mixture, a very neat symbol, a
very neat representation of the Jekyll and Hyde relationship.... In a bystreet, corresponding to another side of
the same block of houses, its geography curiously distorted and concealed by an agglomeration of various
buildings and courts in that particular spot, is the mysterious Hyde side door. Thus in the composite Jekyll building with its mellow and grand front hall there are
corridors leading to Hyde, to the old surgery theatre,
now Jekyll's laboratory, where not so much dissection as
chemical experiments were conducted by the doctor.
Stevenson musters all possible devices, images, intonation, word patterns, and also false scents, to build up
gradually a world in which the strange transformation to
be described in Jekyll's own words will have the impact
of satisfactory and artistic reality upon the reader—or
rather will lead to such a state of mind in which the
reader will not ask himself whether this transformation
is possible or not. Something of the same sort is managed by Dickens in *Bleak House* when by a miracle of
subtle approach and variegated prose he manages to
make real and satisfying the case of the gin-loaded old
man who literally catches fire inside and is burnt to the
ground.

Stevenson's artistic purpose was to make "a fantastic
drama pass in the presence of plain sensible men" in an
atmosphere familiar to the readers of Dickens, in the setting of London's bleak fog, of solemn elderly gentlemen

drinking old port, of ugly faced houses, of family lawyers and devoted butlers, of anonymous vices thriving somewhere behind the solemn square on which Jekyll lives, and of cold mornings and of hansom cabs. Mr. Utterson, Jekyll's lawyer, is "a decent, reticent, likeable, trustworthy, courageous and crusty gentleman; and what such people can accept as 'real,' the readers are supposed also to accept as real." Utterson's friend Enfield is called "unimpressionable," a sturdy young businessman definitely on the dull side (in fact it is this sturdy dullness that brings him and Utterson together). It is this dull Enfield, a man of little imagination and not good at observing things, whom Stevenson selects to tell the beginning of the story. Enfield does not realize that the door on the bystreet which Hyde uses to bring the cheque signed by Jekyll is the door of the laboratory in Jekyll's house. However, Utterson realizes the connection immediately, and the story has started.

Although to Utterson the fanciful was the immodest, Enfield's story leads him, at home, to take from his safe Jekyll's will in his own handwriting (for Utterson had refused to lend the least assistance in the making of it) and to read again its provision: "not only that, in the case of the decease of Henry Jekyll, M.D., D.C.L., L.L.D., F.R.S., etc., all his possessions were to pass into the hands of his 'friend and benefactor Edward Hyde,' but that in case of Dr. Jekyll's 'disappearance or unexplained absence for any period exceeding three calendar months,' the said Edward Hyde should step into the said Henry Jekyll's shoes without further delay and free from any burthen or obligation, beyond the payment of a few small sums to the members of the doctor's household." Utterson had long detested this will, his indignation swelled by his ignorance of Mr. Hyde: "now, by a sudden turn, it was his knowledge [from Enfield's story of the evil small man and the child]. It was already bad enough when the name was but a name of which he could learn no more. It was worse when it began to be clothed upon with detestable attributes; and out of the shifting, insubstantial mists that had so long baffled his eye, there leaped up the sudden, definite presentment of a fiend.

" 'I thought it was madness,' he said, as he replaced the obnoxious paper in the safe, 'and now I begin to fear it is disgrace.' "

Enfield's story about the accident starts to breed in Utterson's mind when he goes to bed. Enfield had begun: "I was coming home from some place at the end of the world, about three o'clock of a black winter morning, and my way lay through a part of town where there was literally nothing to be seen but lamps. Street after street, and all the folks asleep—street after street, all lighted up as if for a procession and all as empty as a church...." (Enfield was a stolid matter-of-fact young man, but Stevenson, the artist, just could not help lending him that phrase about the streets all lighted up, with the folks asleep, and all as empty as a church.) This phrase starts to grow and reecho and mirror and remirror itself in dozing Utterson's head: "Mr. Enfield's tale went by before his mind in a scroll of lighted pictures. He would be aware of the great field of lamps of a nocturnal city; then of the figure of a man walking swiftly; then of a child running from the doctor's; and then these met, and that human Juggernaut trod the child down and passed on regardless of her screams. Or else he would see a room in a rich house, where his friend lay asleep, dreaming and smiling at his dreams; and then the door of that room would be opened, the curtains of the bed plucked apart, the sleeper recalled, and lo! there would stand by his side a figure to whom power was given, and even at that dead hour, he must rise and do its bidding. The figure in these two phases haunted the lawyer all night; and if at any time he dozed over, it was but to see it glide more stealthily through sleeping houses, or move the more swiftly and still the more swiftly, even to dizziness, through wider labyrinths of lamplighted city, and at every street corner crush a child and leave her screaming. And still the figure had no face by which he might know it; even in his dreams, it had no face."

Utterson determines to search him out; at various hours when he is free, he posts himself by the door, and at last he sees Mr. Hyde. "He was small and very plainly dressed, and the look of him, even at that distance, went somehow strongly against the watcher's inclination." (Enfield had remarked: "But there was one curious circumstance. I had taken a loathing to my gentleman at first sight.") Utterson accosts him and after some pretexts he asks to see Hyde's face, which Stevenson carefully does not describe. Utterson does tell the reader other things, however: "Mr. Hyde was pale and dwarfish, he gave an impression of deformity without any nameable malformation, he had a displeasing smile, he had borne himself to the lawyer with a sort of murderous mixture of timidity and boldness, and he spoke with a husky, whispering and somewhat broken voice; all these were points against him, but not all of these together could explain the hitherto unknown disgust, loathing and fear with which Mr. Utterson regarded him.... O my poor old Harry Jekyll, if ever I read Satan's signature upon a face, it is on that of your new friend."

Utterson goes around to the square, rings the bell, and inquires of Poole the butler whether Dr. Jekyll is in, but Poole reports that he has gone out. Utterson asks whether it is right that Hyde should let himself in by the old dissecting-room door when the doctor is out, but the butler reassures him that Hyde has a key by the doctor's permission and that the servants have all been ordered to obey him. "'I do not think I ever met Mr. Hyde?' asked Utterson.

"'O, dear no, sir. He never *dines* here,' replied the butler. 'Indeed we see very little of him on this side of the house; he mostly comes and goes by the laboratory.'"

Utterson suspects blackmail, and determines to help Jekyll if he will be permitted. Shortly the opportunity comes but Jekyll will not be helped. "'You do not understand my position,' returned the doctor, with a certain incoherency of manner. 'I am painfully situated, Utterson; my position is a very strange—a very strange one. It is one of those affairs that cannot be mended by talking.'" He adds, however, "just to put your good heart at rest, I will tell you one thing: the moment I choose, I can be rid of Mr. Hyde. I give you my hand upon that," and the interview closes with Utterson reluctantly agreeing to Jekyll's plea to see that Hyde gets his rights "when I am no longer here."

The Carew murder is the event that begins to bring the story into focus. A servant girl, romantically given, is musing in the moonlight when she perceives a mild and beautiful old gentleman inquiring the way of a certain Mr. Hyde, who had once visited her master and for whom she had conceived a dislike. "He had in his hand a heavy cane, with which he was trifling; but he answered never a word, and seemed to listen with an ill-contained impatience. And then all of a sudden he broke out in a great flame of anger, stamping with his foot, brandishing the cane, and carrying on (as the maid described it) like a madman. The old gentleman took a step back, with the air of one very much surprised and a trifle hurt; and at that Mr. Hyde broke out of all bounds and clubbed him to the earth. And next moment, with ape-like fury, he was trampling his victim under foot and hailing down a storm of blows, under which the bones were audibly shattered and the body jumped upon the roadway. At the horror of these sights and sounds, the maid fainted."

The old man had been carrying a letter addressed to Utterson, who is therefore called upon by a police inspector and identifies the body as that of Sir Danvers Carew. He recognizes the remains of the stick as a cane he had presented to Dr. Jekyll many years before, and he offers to lead the officer to Mr. Hyde's address in Soho, one of the worst parts of London. There are some pretty verbal effects, particularly of alliteration, in the paragraph: "It was by this time about nine in the morning, and the first fog of the season. A great chocolate-coloured pall lowered over heaven, but the wind was continually charging and routing these embattled vapours; so that as the cab crawled from street to street, Mr. Utterson beheld a marvelous number of degrees and hues of twilight; for here it would be dark like the back-end of evening; and light of some strange conflagration; and here, for a moment, the fog would be broken up, and a haggard shaft of daylight would glance in between the swirling wreaths. The dismal quarter of Soho seen under these changing glimpses, with its muddy ways, and slatternly passengers, and its lamps, which had never been extinguished or had been kindled afresh to combat this mournful reinvasion of darkness, seemed, in the lawyer's eyes, like a district of some city in a nightmare."

Hyde is not at home, the flat has been ransacked in great disorder, and it is clear that the murderer has fled. That afternoon Utterson calls on Jekyll and is received in the laboratory: "The fire burned in the grate; a lamp was set lighted on the chimney shelf, for even in the houses the fog began to lie thickly; and there, close up to the warmth, sat Dr. Jekyll, looking deadly sick. He did not rise to meet his visitor, but held out a cold hand and bade him welcome in a changed voice." In response to Utterson's question whether Hyde is in concealment there, " 'Utterson, I swear to God,' cried the doctor, 'I swear to God I will never set eyes on him again. I bind my honour to you that I am done with him in this world. It is all at an end. And indeed he does not want my help; you do not know him as I do; he is safe, he is quite safe; mark my words, he will never more be heard of.' " He shows Utterson a letter signed "Edward Hyde" which signifies that his benefactor need not be concerned since he has means of escape on which he places a sure dependence. Under Utterson's questioning, Jekyll admits that it was Hyde who had dictated the terms of the will and Utterson congratulates him on his escape from being murdered himself. " 'I have had what is far more to the purpose,' returned the doctor solemnly: 'I have had a lesson—O God, Utterson, what a lesson I have had!' And he covered his face for a moment with his hands." From his chief clerk Utterson learns that the hand of the Hyde letter, though sloping in the opposite direction, is very like that of Jekyll. " 'What!' he thought. 'Henry Jekyll forge for a murderer!' And his blood ran cold in his veins."

Stevenson has set himself a difficult artistic problem, and we wonder very much if he is strong enough to solve it. Let us break it up into the following points:

1. In order to make the fantasy plausible he wishes to have it pass through the minds of matter-of-fact persons, Utterson and Enfield, who even for all their commonplace logic must be affected by something bizarre and nightmarish in Hyde.

2. These two stolid souls must convey to the reader something of the horror of Hyde, but at the same

time they, being neither artists nor scientists, unlike Dr. Lanyon, cannot be allowed by the author to notice details.

3. Now if Stevenson makes Enfield and Utterson too commonplace and too plain, they will not be able to express even the vague discomfort Hyde causes them. On the other hand, the reader is curious not only about their reactions but he wishes also to see Hyde's face for himself.

4. But the author himself does not see Hyde's face clearly enough, and could only have it described by Enfield or Utterson in some oblique, imaginative, suggestive way, which, however, would not be a likely manner of expression on the part of these stolid souls.

I suggest that given the situation and the characters, the only way to solve the problem is to have the aspect of Hyde cause in Enfield and Utterson not only a shudder of repulsion but also something else. I suggest that the shock of Hyde's presence brings out the hidden artist in Enfield and the hidden artist in Utterson. Otherwise the bright perceptions that illumine Enfield's story of his journey through the lighted, empty streets before he witnessed Mr. Hyde's assault on the child, and the colorful imaginings of Utterson's dreams after he has heard the story can only be explained by the abrupt intrusion of the author with his own set of artistic values and his own diction and intonation. A curious problem indeed.

There is a further problem. Stevenson gives us the specific, lifelike description of events by humdrum London gentlemen, but contrasting with this are the unspecified, vague, but ominous allusions to pleasures and dreadful vices somewhere behind the scenes. On the one side there is "reality"; on the other, "a nightmare world."

If the author really means there to be a sharp contrast between the two, then the story could strike us as a little disappointing. If we are really being told "never mind what the evil was—just believe it was something very bad," then we might feel ourselves cheated and bullied. We could feel cheated by vagueness in the most interesting part of the story just because its setting is so matter of fact and realistic. The question that must be asked of the work is whether Utterson and the fog and the cabs and the pale butler are more "real" than the weird experiments and unmentionable adventures of Jekyll and Hyde.

Critics such as Stephen Gwynn have noticed a curious flaw in the story's so-called familiar and commonplace setting. "There is a certain characteristic avoidance: the tale, as it develops, might almost be one of a community of monks. Mr. Utterson is a bachelor, so is Jekyll himself, so by all indications is Enfield, the younger man who first brings to Utterson a tale of Hyde's brutalities. So, for that matter, is Jekyll's butler, Poole, whose part in the story is not negligible. Excluding two or three vague servant maids, a conventional hag and a faceless little girl running for a doctor, the gentle sex has no part in the action. It has been suggested that Stevenson, 'working as he did under Victorian restrictions,' and not wishing to bring colours into the story alien to its monkish pattern, consciously refrained from placing a painted feminine mask upon the secret pleasures in which Jekyll indulged."

If, for instance, Stevenson had gone as far as, say, Tolstoy, who was also a Victorian and also did not go very far—but if Stevenson had gone as far as Tolstoy had in depicting the light loves of Oblonski, the French girl, the singer, the little ballerina, etc., it would have been artistically very difficult to have Jekyll-Oblonski exude a Hyde. A certain amiable, jovial, and lighthearted strain running through the pleasures of a gay blade would then have been difficult to reconcile with the medieval rising as a black scarecrow against a livid sky in the guise of Hyde. It was safer for the artist not to be specific and to leave the pleasures of Jekyll undescribed. But does not this safety, this easy way, does it not denote a certain weakness in the artist? I think it does.

First of all, this Victorian reticence prompts the modern reader to grope for conclusions that perhaps Stevenson never intended to be groped for. For instance, Hyde is called Jekyll's protege and his benefactor, but one may be puzzled by the implication of another epithet attached to Hyde, that of Henry Jekyll's favorite, which sounds almost like *minion*. The all-male pattern that Gwynn has mentioned may suggest by a twist of thought that Jekyll's secret adventures were homosexual practices so common in London behind the Victorian veil. Utterson's first supposition is that Hyde blackmails the good doctor—and it is hard to imagine what special grounds for blackmailing would there have been in a bachelor's consorting with ladies of light morals. Or do Utterson and Enfield suspect that Hyde is Jekyll's illegitimate son? "Paying for the capers of his youth" is what Enfield suggests. But the difference in age as implied by the difference in their appearance does not seem to be quite sufficient for Hyde to be Jekyll's son. Moreover, in his will Jekyll calls Hyde his "friend and benefactor," a curious choice of words perhaps bitterly ironic but hardly referring to a son.

In any case, the good reader cannot be quite satisfied with the mist surrounding Jekyll's adventures. And this is especially irritating since Hyde's adventures, likewise anonymous, are supposed to be monstrous exaggerations of Jekyll's wayward whims. Now the only thing that we do guess about Hyde's pleasures is that they are sadistic—he enjoys the infliction of pain. "What Stevenson desired to convey in the person of Hyde was the presence of evil wholly divorced from good. Of all wrongs in the world Stevenson most hated cruelty; and the inhuman brute whom he imagines is shown not in his beastly lusts, whatever they specifically were, but in his savage indifference" to the human beings whom he hurts and kills.

In his essay "A Gossip on Romance" Stevenson has this to say about narrative structure: "The right kind of thing should fall out in the right kind of place; the right kind of thing should follow; and . . . all the circumstances in a tale answer one another likes notes in music. The threads of a story come from time to time together and make a picture in the web; the characters fall from time to time into some attitude to each other or to nature, which stamps the story home like an illustration. Crusoe recoiling from the footprint [*Emma smiling under her iridescent sunshade; Anna reading the shop signs along the road to her death*], these are the culminating moments in the legend, and each has been printed on the mind's eye for ever. Other things we may forget; . . . we may forget the author's comment, although perhaps it was ingenious and true; but these epoch-making scenes which put the last mark of [artistic] truth upon a story and fill up, at one blow, our capacity for [artistic] pleasure, we so adopt into the very bosom of our mind that neither time nor tide can efface or weaken the impression. This, then, is [the highest,] the plastic part of literature: to embody character, thought, or emotion in some act or attitude that shall be remarkably striking to the mind's eye."

"Dr. Jekyll and Mr. Hyde," as a phrase, has entered the language for just the reason of its epoch-making scene, the impression of which cannot be effaced. The scene is, of course, the narrative of Jekyll's transformation into Mr. Hyde which, curiously, has the more impact in that it comes as the explanation contained in two letters after the chronological narrative has come to an end, when Utterson—alerted by Poole that it is someone other than the doctor who for days has immured himself in the laboratory—breaks down the door and finds Hyde in Jekyll's too-large clothes, dead on the floor and with the reek of the cyanide capsule he has just crushed in his teeth. The brief narrative passage between Hyde's murder of Sir Danvers and this discovery merely prepares for the explanation. Time passed but Hyde had disappeared. Jekyll seemed his old self and on the eighth of January gave a small dinner party attended by Utterson and his now reconciled friend, Dr. Lanyon. But four days later Jekyll was not at home to Utterson although they have been seeing each other daily for over two months. On the sixth day when he was refused admission he called on Dr. Lanyon for advice only to find a man with death written on his face, who refused to hear the name of Jekyll. After taking to his bed Dr. Lanyon dies within a week, and Utterson receives a letter in the doctor's hand marked not to be opened before the death or disappearance of Henry Jekyll. A day or two later, Utterson is taking a walk with Enfield, who once again enters the story, and in passing the court on the bystreet they turn in and converse briefly with an ill-looking Jekyll sitting in the window of his laboratory, an interview that ends when "the smile was struck out of [Jekyll's] face and succeeded by an expression of such abject terror and despair, as froze the very blood of the two gentlemen below. They saw it but for a glimpse for the window was instantly thrust down; but that glimpse had been sufficient, and they turned and left the court without a word."

It is not long after that episode that Poole comes to see Mr. Utterson and the action is taken that leads to the forced entry. " 'Utterson,' said the voice, 'for God's sake, have mercy!'

" 'Ah, that's not Jekyll's voice—it's Hyde's!' cried Utterson. 'Down with the door, Poole!'

"Poole swung the axe over his shoulder; the blow shook the building, and the red baize door leaped against the lock and hinges. A dismal screech, as of mere animal terror, rang from the cabinet. Up went the axe again, and again the panels crashed and the frame bounded; four times the blow fell; but the wood was tough and the fittings were of excellent workmanship; and it was not until the fifth, that the lock burst and the wreck of the door fell inwards on the carpet."

At first Utterson thinks that Hyde has killed Jekyll and hidden the body, but a search is fruitless. However, he finds a note from Jekyll on the desk asking him to read Dr. Lanyon's letter and then, if he is still curious, to read the enclosed confession, which Utterson sees is contained in a bulky sealed packet. The narrative proper ends as Utterson, back in his office, breaks the seals and starts to read. The interlocking explanation contained in the narrative-within-a-narrative of the two letters concludes the story.

Briefly, Dr. Lanyon's letter describes how he received an urgent registered letter from Jekyll requesting him to go to the laboratory, to remove a certain drawer containing various chemicals, and to give it to a messenger who would arrive at midnight. He secures the drawer (Poole had also had a registered letter) and returning to his house examines the contents:

[Here Nabokov quoted excerpts from "... when I opened one of the wrappers ... through "upon the table," pp.

102–106. In this passage, Lanyon has retrieved the potion, and Hyde, as messenger, has come to get the potion he so desperately needs. Hyde mixes the potion in front of Lanyon.]

Lanyon is invited to withdraw, or to remain if he is curious so long as what transpires will be kept secret "under the seal of our profession." Lanyon stays. " 'It is well,' replied my visitor. 'Lanyon, you remember your vows: . . . And now, you who have so long been bound to the most narrow and material views, you who have denied the virtue of transcendental medicine, you who have derided your superiors—behold!'

[Here Nabokov continued, quoting from "He put the glass . . ." through "murderer of Carew," pp. 106–107.]

Dr. Lanyon's letter leaves quite enough suspense to be filled in by "Henry Jekyll's Full Statement of the Case" which Utterson then reads, bringing the story to a close. Jekyll recounts how his youthful pleasures, which he concealed, hardened into a profound duplicity of life. "It was thus rather the exacting nature of my aspirations than any particular degradation in my faults, that made me what I was, and, with even a deeper trench than in the majority of men, severed in me those provinces of good and ill which divide and compound man's dual nature." His scientific studies led wholly towards the mystic and the transcendental and drew him steadily toward the truth "that man is not truly one, but truly two." And even before the course of his scientific experiments had "begun to suggest the most naked possibility of such a miracle, I had learned to dwell with pleasure, as a beloved daydream, on the thought of the separation of these elements. If each, I told myself, could be housed in separate identities, life would be relieved of all that was unbearable; the unjust might go his way, delivered from the aspirations and remorse of his more upright twin; and the just could walk steadfastly and securely on his upward path, doing the good things in which he found his pleasure, and no longer exposed to disgrace and penitence by the hands of this extraneous evil. It was the curse of mankind that these incongruous faggots were thus bound together—that in the agonised womb of consciousness, these polar twins should be continually struggling. How, then, were they dissociated?"

We then have the vivid description of his discovery of the potion and, in testing it, the emergence of Mr. Hyde who, "alone in the ranks of mankind, was pure evil." "I lingered but a moment at the mirror; the second and conclusive experiment had yet to be attempted; it yet remained to be seen if I had lost my identity beyond redemption and must flee before daylight from a house that was no longer mine; and hurrying back to my cabinet, I once more prepared and drank the cup, once more suffered the pangs of dissolution, and came to myself once more with the character, the stature and the face of Henry Jekyll."

For a time all is well. "I was the first that could plod in the public eye with a load of genial respectability, and in a moment, like a schoolboy, strip off these lendings and spring headlong into the sea of liberty. But for me, in my impenetrable mantle, the safety was complete. Think of it—I did not even exist! Let me but escape into my laboratory door, give me but a second or two to mix and swallow the draught that I had always standing ready; and whatever he had done, Edward Hyde would pass away like the stain of breath upon a mirror; and there in his stead, quietly at home, trimming the midnight lamp in his study, a man who could afford to laugh at suspicion, would be Henry Jekyll." The pleasures Jekyll experiences as Mr. Hyde, while his own conscience slumbered, are passed over without detail except that what in Jekyll had been "undignified; I would scarce use a harder term," in the person of Hyde "began to turn toward the monstrous. . . . This familiar that I called out of my own soul, and sent forth alone to do his good pleasure, was a being inherently malign and villainous; his every act and thought centered on self; drinking pleasure with bestial avidity from any degree of torture to another; relentless like a man of stone." Hyde's sadism is thus established.

Then things begin to go wrong. It becomes harder and harder to return to Jekyll from the person of Hyde. Sometimes a double dose of the elixir is required, and once at the risk of life, a triple dose. On one occasion there was total failure. Then one morning Jekyll woke up in his own bed in the house on the square and lazily began to examine the illusion that somehow he was in Hyde's house in Soho.

[Here Nabokov quoted from "I was still so engaged . . ." through "I had awakened Edward Hyde," p. 116.]

He manages to make his way to the laboratory and to restore his Jekyll shape, but the shock of the unconscious transformation goes deep, and he determines to forsake his double existence. "Yes, I preferred the elderly and discontented doctor, surrounded by friends and cherishing honest hopes [*observe the alliteration in this passage*]; and bade a resolute farewell to the liberty, the comparative youth, the light step, leaping impulses and secret pleasures, that I had enjoyed in the disguise of Hyde."

For two months Jekyll persists in this resolution, although he does not give up his house in Soho or Hyde's smaller clothing that lies ready in his laboratory. Then he weakens. "My devil had been long caged, he came out roaring. I was conscious, even when I took the draught of a more unbridled, a more furious propensity to ill." In this furious mood he murders Sir Danvers Carew, stirred to rage by the old man's civilities. After his transports of glee as he mauls the body, a cold thrill of terror disperses the mists.

[Here Nabokov quoted from "I saw my life to be for-feit . . ." through "his clasped hands to God," p. 120.]

With a sense of joy Jekyll sees that his problem is solved and that he dare never again assume the form of the wanted murderer Hyde. For several months he lives a life of exemplary good works, but he was still cursed with duality of purpose and "the lower side of me, so long indulged, so recently chained down, began to growl for license." In his own person, for he can never again risk Hyde, he begins to pursue his secret vices. This brief excursion into evil finally destroyed the balance of his soul. One day, sitting in Regent's Park, "a qualm came over me, a horrid nausea and the most deadly shudder-ing. These passed away, and left me faint; and then as in its turn faintness subsided, I began to be aware of a change in the temper of my thoughts, a greater boldness, a contempt of danger, a solution of the bonds of obliga-tion. I looked down; my clothes hung formlessly on my shrunken limbs; the hand that lay on my knees was corded and hairy. I was once more Edward Hyde. A mo-ment before I had been safe of all men's respect, wealthy, beloved—the cloth laying for me in the dining-room at home; and now I was the common quarry of mankind, hunted, houseless, a known murderer, thrall to the gal-lows." As Hyde he cannot return to his house, and so he is forced into the expedient of calling on Dr. Lanyon's help, described in the doctor's letter.

The end now comes with rapidity. The very next morning, crossing the court of his own house, he is again seized by the vertigo of change and it took a double dose to restore him to himself. Six hours later the pangs returned and he had to drink the potion once more. From that time on he was never safe and it required the constant stimulation of the drug to enable him to keep the shape of Jekyll. (It was at one of these moments that Enfield and Utterson conversed with him at the window on the court, a meeting abruptly terminated by the onset of a transformation.) "At all hours of the day and night, I would be taken with the premonitory shudder; above all, if I slept, or even dozed for a moment in my chair, it was always as Hyde that I awakened.

[Here Nabokov continued, quoting from "Under the strain of this . . ." through "heart to pity him," pp. 125–26.]

The last calamity falls when the provision of the special salt for his potion begins to run low; when he sends for a fresh order the first change of color occurred but not the second, and no transformation took place. Poole had testified to Utterson of the desperate search for another supply.

[Here Nabokov quoted from "All this last week . . ." through "returned Poole," pp. 89–90.]

Convinced at last that his first supply was impure, that it was the unknown impurity which gave efficacy to the draught, and that he can never renew his supply, Jekyll begins to write the confession and a week later is finishing it under the influence of the last of the old powders. "This, then, is the last time, short of a miracle, that Henry Jekyll can think his own thoughts or see his own face (now how sadly altered!) in the glass." He hastens to conclude lest Hyde suddenly take over and tear the papers to shreds. "Half an hour from now, when I shall again and forever reindue that hated personality, I know how I shall sit shuddering and weeping in my chair, or continue, with the most strained and fearstruck ecstasy of listening, to pace up and down this room (my last earthly refuge) and give ear to every sound of men- ace. Will Hyde die upon the scafford? Or will he find courage to release himself at the last moment? God knows; I am careless; this is my true hour of death, and what is to follow concerns another than myself. Here then, as I lay down the pen and proceed to seal up my confession, I bring the life of that unhappy Henry Jekyll to an end."

I would like to say a few words about Stevenson's last moments. As you know by now, I am not one to go heav- ily for the human interest stuff when speaking of books. Human interest is not in my line, as Vronski used to say. But books have their destiny, according to the Latin tag, and sometimes the destinies of authors follow those of their books. There is old Tolstoy in 1910 abandoning his family to wander away and die in a station master's room to the rumble of passing trains that had killed Anna Kar- enin. And there is something in Stevenson's death in 1894 on Samoa, imitating in a curious way the wine theme and the transformation theme of his fantasy. He went down to the cellar to fetch a bottle of his favorite burgundy, uncorked it in the kitchen, and suddenly cried out to his wife: what's the matter with me, what is this strangeness, has my face changed?—and fell on the floor.

A blood vessel had burst in his brain and it was all over in a couple of hours.

What, has my face changed? There is a curious thematical link between this last episode in Stevenson's life and the fateful transformations in his most wonderful book.

—Vladimir Nabokov

DR. JEKYLL AND MR. HYDE

STORY OF THE DOOR

Mr. Utterson the lawyer was a man of a rugged countenance that was never lighted by a smile; cold, scanty and embarrassed in discourse; backward in sentiment; lean, long, dusty, dreary and yet somehow lovable. At friendly meetings, and when the wine was to his taste, something eminently human beaconed from his eye; something indeed which never found its way into his talk, but which spoke not only in these silent symbols of the after-dinner face, but more often and loudly in the acts of his life. He was austere with himself; drank gin when he was alone, to mortify a taste for vintages; and though he enjoyed the theatre, had not crossed the doors of one for twenty years. But he had an approved tolerance for others; sometimes wondering, almost with envy, at the high pressure of spirits involved in their misdeeds; and in any extremity inclined to help rather than to reprove. "I incline to Cain's heresy," he used to say quaintly: "I let my brother go to the devil in his own way." In this character, it was frequently his fortune to be the last reputable acquaintance and the last good influence in the lives of downgoing men. And to such as these, so long as they came about his chambers, he never marked a shade of change in his demeanour.

No doubt the feat was easy to Mr. Utterson; for he was undemonstrative at the best, and even his friendship seemed to be founded in a similar catholicity of good-nature. It is the mark of a modest man to accept his friendly circle ready-made from the hands of opportunity; and that was the lawyer's way. His friends were those of his own blood or those whom he had known the longest; his affections, like ivy, were the growth of time, they implied no aptness in the object. Hence, no doubt, the bond that united him to Mr. Richard Enfield, his distant kinsman, the well-known man about town. It was a nut to crack for many, what these two could see in each other, or what subject they could find in common. It was reported by those who encountered them in their Sunday walks, that they said nothing, looked singularly dull, and would hail with obvious relief the appearance of a friend. For all that, the two men put the greatest store by these excursions, counted them the chief jewel of each week, and not only set aside occasions of pleasure, but even resisted the calls of business, that they might enjoy them uninterrupted.

It chanced on one of these rambles that their way led them down a by-street in a busy quarter of London. The street was small and what is called quiet, but it drove a thriving trade on the week-days. The inhabitants were all doing well, it seemed, and all emulously hoping to do better still, and laying out the surplus of their grains in coquetry; so that the shop fronts stood along that thoroughfare with an air of invitation, like rows of smiling saleswomen. Even on Sunday, when it veiled its more florid charms and lay comparatively empty of passage, the street shone out in contrast to its dingy neighbourhood, like a fire in a forest; and with its freshly painted shutters, well-polished brasses, and general cleanliness and gaiety of note, instantly caught and pleased the eye of the passenger.

Two doors from one corner, on the left h
east, the line was broken by the entry of a cou
at that point, a certain sinister block of buildin
forward its gable on the street. It was two storeys high;
showed no window, nothing but a door on the lower storey and a blind forehead of discoloured wall on the upper; and bore in every feature, the marks of prolonged
and sordid negligence. The door, which was equipped
with neither bell nor knocker, was blistered and dis-
tained. Tramps slouched into the recess and struck
matches on the panels; children kept shop upon the
steps; the schoolboy had tried his knife on the mould-
ings; and for close on a generation, no one had appeared
to drive away these random visitors or to repair their
ravages.

Mr. Enfield and the lawyer were on the other side of
the by-street; but when they came abreast of the entry,
the former lifted up his cane and pointed.

"Did you ever remark that door?" he asked; and
when his companion had replied in the affirmative, "It is
connected in my mind," added he, "with a very odd
story."

"Indeed?" said Mr. Utterson, with a slight change of
voice, "and what was that?"

"Well, it was this way," returned Mr. Enfield: "I was
coming home from some place at the end of the world,
about three o'clock of a black winter morning, and my
way lay through a part of town where there was literally
nothing to be seen but lamps. Street after street, and all
the folks asleep—street after street, all lighted up as if
for a procession and all as empty as a church—till at last
I got into that state of mind when a man listens and listens and begins to long for the sight of a policeman. All
at once, I saw two figures: one a little man who was
stumping along eastward at a good walk, and the other a

girl of maybe eight or ten was running as hard as she was able down a cross street. Well, sir, the two ran into one another naturally enough at the corner; and then came the horrible part of the thing; for the man trampled calmly over the child's body and left her screaming on the ground. It sounds nothing to hear, but it was hellish to see. It wasn't like a man; it was like some damned Juggernaut. I gave a view halloa, took to my heels, collared my gentleman, and brought him back to where there was already quite a group about the screaming child. He was perfectly cool and made no resistance, but gave me one look, so ugly that it brought out the sweat on me like running. The people who had turned out were the girl's own family; and pretty soon, the doctor, for whom she had been sent, put in his appearance. Well, the child was not much the worse, more frightened, according to the Sawbones; and there you might have supposed would be an end to it. But there was one curious circumstance. I had taken a loathing to my gentleman at first sight. So had the child's family, which was only natural. But the doctor's case was what struck me. He was the usual cut and dry apothecary, of no particular age and colour, with a strong Edinburgh accent, and about as emotional as a bagpipe. Well, sir, he was like the rest of us; every time he looked at my prisoner, I saw that Sawbones turn sick and white with desire to kill him. I knew what was in his mind, just as he knew what was in mine; and killing being out of the question, we did the next best. We told the man we could and would make such a scandal out of this, as should make his name stink from one end of London to the other. If he had any friends or any credit, we undertook that he should lose them. And all the time, as we were pitching it in red hot, we were keeping the women off him as best we could, for they were as wild as harpies. I never saw a circle of such hateful faces; and there was the man in the middle, with a kind of black, sneering coolness—frightened too, I could see that—but carrying it off, sir, really like Satan. 'If you choose to make capital out of this accident,' said he, 'I am naturally helpless. No gentleman but wishes to avoid a scene,' says he. 'Name your figure.' Well, we screwed him up to a hundred pounds for the child's family; he would have clearly liked to stick out; but there was something about the lot of us that meant mischief, and at last he struck. The next thing was to get the money; and where do you think he carried us but to that place with the door?—whipped out a key, went in, and presently came back with the matter of ten pounds in gold and a cheque for the balance on Coutts's, drawn payable to bearer and signed with a name that I can't mention, though it's one of the points of my story, but it was a name at least very well known and often printed. The figure was stiff; but the signature was good for more than that, if it was only genuine. I took the liberty of pointing out to my gentleman that the whole business looked apocryphal, and that a man does not, in real life, walk into a cellar door at four in the morning and come out with another man's cheque for close upon a hundred pounds. But he was quite easy and sneering. 'Set your mind at rest,' says he, 'I will stay with you till the banks open and cash the cheque myself.' So we all set off, the doctor, and the child's father, and our friend and myself, and passed the rest of the night in my chambers; and next day, when we had breakfasted, went in a body to the bank. I gave in the cheque myself, and said I had every reason to believe it was a forgery. Not a bit of it. The cheque was genuine."

"Tut-tut," said Mr. Utterson.

"I see you feel as I do," said Mr. Enfield. "Yes, it's a bad story. For my man was a fellow that nobody could have to do with, a really damnable man; and the person that drew the cheque is the very pink of the proprieties, celebrated too, and (what makes it worse) one of your fellows who do what they call good. Black-mail, I suppose; an honest man paying through the nose for some of the capers of his youth. Black-Mail House is what I call the place with the door, in consequence. Though even that, you know, is far from explaining all," he added, and with the words fell into a vein of musing.

From this he was recalled by Mr. Utterson asking rather suddenly: "And you don't know if the drawer of the cheque lives there?"

"A likely place, isn't it?" returned Mr. Enfield. "But I happen to have noticed his address; he lives in some square or another."

"And you never asked about the—place with the door?" said Mr. Utterson.

"No, sir: I had a delicacy," was the reply. "I feel very strongly about putting questions; it partakes too much of the style of the day of judgment. You start a question, and it's like starting a stone. You sit quietly on the top of a hill; and away the stone goes, starting others; and presently some bland old bird (the last you would have thought of) is knocked on the head in his own back garden and the family have to change their name. No, sir, I make it a rule of mine: the more it looks like Queer Street, the less I ask."

"A very good rule, too," said the lawyer.

"But I have studied the place for myself," continued Mr. Enfield. "It seems scarcely a house. There is no other door, and nobody goes in or out of that one but, once in a great while, the gentleman of my adventure. There are three windows looking on the court on the first floor; none below; the windows are always shut but they're clean. And then there is a chimney which is generally smoking; so somebody must live there. And yet it's not so sure; for the buildings are so packed together about the court, that it's hard to say where one ends and another begins."

The pair walked on again for a while in silence; and then, "Enfield," said Mr. Utterson, "that's a good rule of yours."

"Yes, I think it is," returned Enfield.

"But for all that," continued the lawyer, "there's one point I want to ask: I want to ask the name of that man who walked over the child."

"Well," said Mr. Enfield, "I can't see what harm it would do. It was a man of the name of Hyde."

"Hm," said Mr. Utterson. "What sort of a man is he to see?"

"He is not easy to describe. There is something wrong with his appearance; something displeasing, something down-right detestable. I never saw a man I so disliked, and yet I scarce know why. He must be deformed somewhere; he gives a strong feeling of deformity, although I couldn't specify the point. He's an extraordinary looking man, and yet I really can name nothing out of the way. No, sir; I can make no hand of it; I can't describe him. And it's not want of memory; for I declare I can see him this moment."

Mr. Utterson again walked some way in silence and obviously under a weight of consideration. "You are sure he used a key?" he inquired at last.

"My dear sir . . ." began Enfield, surprised out of himself.

"Yes, I know," said Utterson; "I know it must seem strange. The fact is, if I do not ask you the name of the other party, it is because I know it already. You see, Richard, your tale has gone home. If you have been inexact in any point, you had better correct it."

"I think you might have warned me," returned the

other with a touch of sullenness. "But I have been pedantically exact, as you call it. The fellow had a key; and what's more, he has it still. I saw him use it, not a week ago."

Mr. Utterson sighed deeply but said never a word; and the young man presently resumed. "Here is another lesson to say nothing," said he. "I am ashamed of my long tongue. Let us make a bargain never to refer to this again."

"With all my heart," said the lawyer. "I shake hands on that, Richard."

SEARCH FOR MR. HYDE

That evening Mr. Utterson came home to his bachelor house in sombre spirits and sat down to dinner without relish. It was his custom of a Sunday, when this meal was over, to sit close by the fire, a volume of some dry divinity on his reading desk, until the clock of the neighbouring church rang out the hour of twelve, when he would go soberly and gratefully to bed. On this night, however, as soon as the cloth was taken away, he took up a candle and went into his business room. There he opened his safe, took from the most private part of it a document endorsed on the envelope as Dr. Jekyll's Will, and sat down with a clouded brow to study its contents. The will was holograph, for Mr. Utterson, though he took charge of it now that it was made, had refused to lend the least assistance in the making of it; it provided not only that, in case of the decease of Henry Jekyll, M.D., D.C.L., L.L.D., F.R.S., etc., all his possessions were to pass into the hands of his "friend and benefactor Edward Hyde," but that in case of Dr. Jekyll's "disappearance or unexplained absence for any period exceeding three calendar months," the said Edward Hyde should step into the said Henry Jekyll's shoes without further delay and free from any burthen or obligation, beyond the payment of a few small sums to the members of the doctor's household. This document had long been the lawyer's eyesore. It offended him both as a lawyer and as a lover of the sane and customary sides of life, to whom the fanciful was the immodest. And hitherto it was his ignorance of Mr. Hyde that had swelled his indignation; now, by a sudden turn, it was his knowledge. It was already bad enough when the name was but a name of which he could learn no more. It was worse when it began to be clothed upon with detestable attributes; and out of the shifting, insubstantial mists that had so long baffled his eye, there leaped up the sudden, definite presentment of a fiend.

"I thought it was madness," he said, as he replaced the obnoxious paper in the safe, "and now I begin to fear it is disgrace."

With that he blew out his candle, put on a greatcoat and set forth in the direction of Cavendish Square, that citadel of medicine, where his friend, the great Dr. Lanyon, had his house and received his crowding patients. "If anyone knows, it will be Lanyon," he had thought.

The solemn butler knew and welcomed him; he was subjected to no stage of delay, but ushered direct from the door to the dining-room where Dr. Lanyon sat alone over his wine. This was a hearty, healthy, dapper, red-faced gentleman, with a shock of hair prematurely white, and a boisterous and decided manner. At sight of Mr. Utterson, he sprang up from his chair and welcomed him with both hands. The geniality, as was the way of the man, was somewhat theatrical to the eye; but it reposed on genuine feeling. For these two were old friends, old mates both at school and college, both thorough respecters of themselves and of each other, and what does not always follow, men who thoroughly enjoyed each other's company.

After a little rambling talk, the lawyer led up to the subject which so disagreeably preoccupied his mind.

"I suppose, Lanyon," said he, "you and I must be the two oldest friends that Henry Jekyll has?"

"I wish the friends were younger," chuckled Dr. Lanyon. "But I suppose we are. And what of that? I see little of him now."

"Indeed?" said Utterson. "I thought you had a bond of common interest."

"We had," was the reply. "But it is more than ten years since Henry Jekyll became too fanciful for me. He began to go wrong, wrong in mind; and though of course I continue to take an interest in him for old sake's sake, as they say, I see and I have seen devilish little of the man. Such unscientific balderdash," added the doctor, flushing suddenly purple, "would have estranged Damon and Pythias."

This little spirit of temper was somewhat of a relief to Mr. Utterson. "They have only differed on some point of science," he thought; and being a man of no scientific passions (except in the matter of conveyancing), he even added: "It is nothing worse than that!" He gave his friend a few seconds to recover his composure, and then approached the question he had come to put. "Did you ever come across a protégé of his—one Hyde?" he asked.

"Hyde?" repeated Lanyon. "No. Never heard of him. Since my time."

That was the amount of information that the lawyer carried back with him to the great, dark bed on which he tossed to and fro, until the small hours of the morning began to grow large. It was a night of little ease to his toiling mind, toiling in mere darkness and besieged by questions.

Six o'clock struck on the bells of the church that was

so conveniently near to Mr. Utterson's dwelling, and still he was digging at the problem. Hitherto it had touched him on the intellectual side alone; but now his imagination also was engaged, or rather enslaved; and as he lay and tossed in the gross darkness of the night and the curtained room, Mr. Enfield's tale went by before his mind in a scroll of lighted pictures. He would be aware of the great field of lamps of a nocturnal city; then of the figure of a man walking swiftly; then of a child running from the doctor's; and then these met, and that human Juggernaut trod the child down and passed on regardless of her screams. Or else he would see a room in a rich house, where his friend lay asleep, dreaming and smiling at his dreams; and then the door of that room would be opened, the curtains of the bed plucked apart, the sleeper recalled, and lo! there would stand by his side a figure to whom power was given, and even at that dead hour, he must rise and do its bidding. The figure in these two phases haunted the lawyer all night; and if at any time he dozed over, it was but to see it glide more stealthily through sleeping houses, or move the more swiftly and still the more swiftly, even to dizziness, through wider labyrinths of lamp-lighted city, and at every street corner crush a child and leave her screaming. And still the figure had no face by which he might know it; even in his dreams, it had no face, or one that baffled him and melted before his eyes; and thus it was that there sprang up and grew apace in the lawyer's mind a singularly strong, almost an inordinate, curiosity to behold the features of the real Mr. Hyde. If he could but once set eyes on him, he thought the mystery would lighten and perhaps roll altogether away, as was the habit of mysterious things when well examined. He might see a reason for his friend's strange preference or bondage (call it which you please) and even for the startling clause of the will.

At least it would be a face worth seeing: the face of a man who was without bowels of mercy: a face which had but to show itself to raise up, in the mind of the unimpressionable Enfield, a spirit of enduring hatred.

From that time forward, Mr. Utterson began to haunt the door in the by-street of shops. In the morning before office hours, at noon when business was plenty, and time scarce, at night under the face of the fogged city moon, by all lights and at all hours of solitude or concourse, the lawyer was to be found on his chosen post.

"If he be Mr. Hyde," he had thought, "I shall be Mr. Seek."

And at last his patience was rewarded. It was a fine dry night; frost in the air; the street as clean as a ballroom floor; the lamps, unshaken by any wind, drawing a regular pattern of light and shadow. By ten o'clock, when the shops were closed, the by-street was very solitary and, in spite of the low growl of London from all round, very silent. Small sounds carried far; domestic sounds out of the houses were clearly audible on either side of the roadway; and the rumour of the approach of any passenger preceded him by a long time. Mr. Utterson had been some minutes at his post, when he was aware of an odd, light footstep drawing near. In the course of his nightly patrols, he had long grown accustomed to the quaint effect with which the footfalls of a single person, while he is still a great way off, suddenly spring out distinct from the vast hum and clatter of the city. Yet his attention had never before been so sharply and decisively arrested; and it was with a strong, superstitious prevision of success that he withdrew into the entry of the court.

The steps drew swiftly nearer, and swelled out suddenly louder as they turned the end of the street. The lawyer, looking forth from the entry, could soon see what manner of man he had to deal with. He was small and very plainly dressed, and the look of him, even at that distance, went somehow strongly against the watcher's inclination. But he made straight for the door, crossing the roadway to save time; and as he came, he drew a key from his pocket like one approaching home.

Mr. Utterson stepped out and touched him on the shoulder as he passed. "Mr. Hyde, I think?"

Mr. Hyde shrank back with a hissing intake of the breath. But his fear was only momentary; and though he did not look the lawyer in the face, he answered coolly enough: "That is my name. What do you want?"

"I see you are going in," returned the lawyer. "I am an old friend of Dr. Jekyll's—Mr. Utterson of Gaunt Street—you must have heard of my name; and meeting you so conveniently, I thought you might admit me."

"You will not find Dr. Jekyll; he is from home," replied Mr. Hyde, blowing in the key. And then suddenly, but without looking up, "How did you know me?" he asked.

"On your side," said Mr. Utterson, "will you do me a favour?"

"With pleasure," replied the other. "What shall it be?"

"Will you let me see your face?" asked the lawyer.

Mr. Hyde appeared to hesitate, and then, as if upon some sudden reflection, fronted about with an air of defiance; and the pair stared at each other pretty fixedly for a few seconds. "Now I shall know you again," said Mr. Utterson. "It may be useful."

"Yes," returned Mr. Hyde, "it is as well we have met; and *à propos,* you should have my address." And he gave a number of a street in Soho.

"Good God!" thought Mr. Utterson, "can he, too, have been thinking of the will?" But he kept his feelings to himself and only grunted in acknowledgment of the address.

"And now," said the other, "how did you know me?"

"By description," was the reply.

"Whose description?"

"We have common friends," said Mr. Utterson.

"Common friends?" echoed Mr. Hyde, a little hoarsely. "Who are they?"

"Jekyll, for instance," said the lawyer.

"He never told you," cried Mr. Hyde, with a flush of anger. "I did not think you would have lied."

"Come," said Mr. Utterson, "that is not fitting language."

The other snarled aloud into a savage laugh; and the next moment with extraordinary quickness, he had unlocked the door and disappeared into the house.

The lawyer stood awhile when Mr. Hyde had left him, the picture of disquietude. Then he began slowly to mount the street, pausing every step or two and putting his hand to his brow like a man in mental perplexity. The problem he was thus debating as he walked, was one of a class that is rarely solved. Mr. Hyde was pale and dwarfish, he gave an impression of deformity without any nameable malformation, he had a displeasing smile, he had borne himself to the lawyer with a sort of murderous mixture of timidity and boldness, and he spoke with a husky, whispering and somewhat broken voice; all these were points against him, but not all of these together could explain the hitherto unknown disgust, loathing and fear with which Mr. Utterson regarded him. "There must be something else," said the perplexed gentleman. "There *is* something more, if I could find a name for it. God bless me, the man seems hardly human! Something troglodytic, shall we say? or can it be the old story of Dr. Fell? or is it the mere radiance of a foul soul that thus transpires through, and transfigures, its clay continent? The last, I think; for, O my poor old Harry

Jekyll, if ever I read Satan's signature upon a face, it is on that of your new friend."

Round the corner from the by-street, there was a square of ancient, handsome houses, now for the most part decayed from their high estate and let in flats and chambers to all sorts and conditions of men; map-engravers, architects, shady lawyers and the agents of obscure enterprises. One house, however, second from the corner, was still occupied entire; and at the door of this, which wore a great air of wealth and comfort, though it was now plunged in darkness except for the fanlight, Mr. Utterson stopped and knocked. A well-dressed, elderly servant opened the door.

"Is Dr. Jekyll at home, Poole?" asked the lawyer.

"I will see, Mr. Utterson," said Poole, admitting the visitor, as he spoke, into a large, low-roofed, comfortable hall, paved with flags, warmed (after the fashion of a country house) by a bright, open fire, and furnished with costly cabinets of oak. "Will you wait here by the fire, sir? or shall I give you a light in the dining-room?"

"Here, thank you," said the lawyer, and he drew near and leaned on the tall fender. This hall, in which he was now left alone, was a pet fancy of his friend the doctor's; and Utterson himself was wont to speak of it as the pleasantest room in London. But tonight there was a shudder in his blood; the face of Hyde sat heavy on his memory; he felt (what was rare with him) a nausea and distaste of life; and in the gloom of his spirits, he seemed to read a menace in the flickering of the firelight on the polished cabinets and the uneasy starting of the shadow on the roof. He was ashamed of his relief, when Poole presently returned to announce that Dr. Jekyll was gone out.

"I saw Mr. Hyde go in by the old dissecting-room door, Poole," he said. "Is that right, when Dr. Jekyll is from home?"

"Quite right, Mr. Utterson, sir," replied the servant. "Mr. Hyde has a key."

"Your master seems to repose a great deal of trust in that young man, Poole," resumed the other musingly.

"Yes, sir, he does indeed," said Poole. "We have all orders to obey him."

"I do not think I ever met Mr. Hyde?" asked Utterson.

"O, dear no, sir. He never *dines* here," replied the butler. "Indeed we see very little of him on this side of the house; he mostly comes and goes by the laboratory."

"Well, good-night, Poole."

"Good-night, Mr. Utterson."

And the lawyer set out homeward with a very heavy heart. "Poor Harry Jekyll," he thought, "my mind misgives me he is in deep waters! He was wild when he was young; a long while ago to be sure; but in the law of God, there is no statute of limitations. Ay, it must be that; the ghost of some old sin, the cancer of some concealed disgrace: punishment coming, *pede claudo,* years after memory has forgotten and self-love condoned the fault." And the lawyer, scared by the thought, brooded awhile on his own past, groping in all the corners of memory, lest by chance some Jack-in-the-Box of an old iniquity should leap to light there. His past was fairly blameless; few men could read the rolls of their life with less apprehension; yet he was humbled to the dust by the many ill things he had done, and raised up again into a sober and fearful gratitude by the many he had come so near to doing, yet avoided. And then by a return on his former subject, he conceived a spark of hope. "This Master Hyde, if he were studied," thought he, "must have secrets of his own; black secrets, by the look of him; secrets compared to which poor Jekyll's worst would be like sunshine. Things cannot continue as they are. It turns me cold to think of this creature stealing like a thief to Harry's bedside; poor Harry, what a wakening! And the danger of it; for if this Hyde suspects the existence of the will, he may grow impatient to inherit. Ay, I must put my shoulders to the wheel—if Jekyll will but let me," he added, "if Jekyll will only let me." For once more he saw before his mind's eye, as clear as transparency, the strange clauses of the will.

Dr. Jekyll Was Quite at Ease

A fortnight later, by excellent good fortune, the doctor gave one of his pleasant dinners to some five or six old cronies, all intelligent, reputable men and all judges of good wine; and Mr. Utterson so contrived that he remained behind after the others had departed. This was no new arrangement, but a thing that had befallen many scores of times. Where Utterson was liked, he was liked well. Hosts loved to detain the dry lawyer, when the lighthearted and loose-tongued had already their foot on the threshold; they liked to sit awhile in his unobtrusive company, practising for solitude, sobering their minds in the man's rich silence after the expense and strain of gaiety. To this rule, Dr. Jekyll was no exception; and as he now sat on the opposite side of the fire—a large, well-made, smooth-faced man of fifty, with something of a slyish cast perhaps, but every mark of capacity and kindness—you could see by his looks that he cherished for Mr. Utterson a sincere and warm affection.

"I have been wanting to speak to you, Jekyll," began the latter. "You know that will of yours?"

A close observer might have gathered that the topic was distasteful; but the doctor carried it off gaily. "My poor Utterson," said he, "you are unfortunate in such a client. I never saw a man so distressed as you were by my will; unless it were that hide-bound pedant, Lanyon, at what he called my scientific heresies. Oh, I know he's a good fellow—you needn't frown—an excellent fellow, and I always mean to see more of him; but a hide-bound pedant for all that; an ignorant, blatant pedant. I was never more disappointed in any man than Lanyon."

"You know I never approved of it," pursued Utterson, ruthlessly disregarding the fresh topic.

"My will? Yes, certainly, I know that," said the doctor, a trifle sharply. "You have told me so."

"Well, I tell you so again," continued the lawyer. "I have been learning something of young Hyde."

The large handsome face of Dr. Jekyll grew pale to the very lips, and there came a blackness about his eyes. "I do not care to hear more," said he. "This is a matter I thought we had agreed to drop."

"What I heard was abominable," said Utterson.

"It can make no change. You do not understand my position," returned the doctor, with a certain incoherency of manner. "I am painfully situated, Utterson; my position is a very strange—a very strange one. It is one of those affairs that cannot be mended by talking."

"Jekyll," said Utterson, "you know me: I am a man to be trusted. Make a clean breast of this in confidence; and I make no doubt I can get you out of it."

"My good Utterson," said the doctor, "this is very good of you, this is downright good of you, and I cannot find words to thank you in. I believe you fully; I would trust you before any man alive, ay, before myself, if I could make the choice; but indeed it isn't what you fancy; it is not as bad as that; and just to put your heart at rest, I will tell you one thing: the moment I choose, I can be rid of Mr. Hyde. I give you my hand upon that; and I thank you again and again; and I will just add one little word, Utterson, that I'm sure you'll take in good part: this is a private matter, and I beg of you to let it sleep."

Utterson reflected a little, looking in the fire.

"I have no doubt you are perfectly right," he said at last, getting to his feet.

"Well, but since we have touched upon this business, and for the last time I hope," continued the doctor, "there is one point I should like you to understand. I have really a very great interest in poor Hyde. I know you have seen him; he told me so; and I fear he was rude. But I do sincerely take a great, a very great interest in that young man; and if I am taken away, Utterson, I wish you to promise me that you will bear with him and get his rights for him. I think you would, if you knew all; and it would be a weight off my mind if you would promise."

"I can't pretend that I shall ever like him," said the lawyer.

"I don't ask that," pleaded Jekyll, laying his hand upon the other's arm; "I only ask for justice; I only ask you to help him for my sake, when I am no longer here."

Utterson heaved an irrepressible sigh. "Well," said he, "I promise."

The Carew Murder Case

Nearly a year later, in the month of October, 18—, London was startled by a crime of singular ferocity and rendered all the more notable by the high position of the victim. The details were few and startling. A maid servant living alone in a house not far from the river, had gone upstairs to bed about eleven. Although a fog rolled over the city in the small hours, the early part of the night was cloudless, and the lane, which the maid's window overlooked, was brilliantly lit by the full moon. It seems she was romantically given, for she sat down upon her box, which stood immediately under the window, and fell into a dream of musing. Never (she used to say, with streaming tears, when she narrated that experience), never had she felt more at peace with all men or thought more kindly of the world. And as she so sat she became aware of an aged beautiful gentleman with white hair, drawing near along the lane; and advancing to meet him, another and very small gentleman, to whom at first she paid less attention. When they had come within speech (which was just under the maid's eyes) the older man bowed and accosted the other with a very pretty manner of politeness. It did not seem as if the subject of his address were of great importance; indeed, from his pointing, it sometimes appeared as if he were only inquiring his way; but the moon shone on his face as he spoke, and the girl was pleased to watch it, it seemed to breathe such an innocent and old-world kindness of disposition, yet with something high too, as of a well-founded self-content. Presently her eye wandered to the other, and she was surprised to recognise in him a certain Mr. Hyde, who had once visited her master and for whom she had conceived a dislike. He had in his hand a heavy cane, with which he was trifling; but he answered never a word, and seemed to listen with an ill-contained impatience. And then all of a sudden he broke out in a great flame of anger, stamping with his foot, brandishing the cane, and carrying on (as the maid described it) like a madman. The old gentleman took a step back, with the air of one very much surprised and a trifle hurt; and at that Mr. Hyde broke out of all bounds and clubbed him to the earth. And next moment, with ape-like fury, he was trampling his victim under foot and hailing down a storm of blows, under which the bones were audibly shattered and the body jumped upon the roadway. At the horror of these sights and sounds, the maid fainted.

It was two o'clock when she came to herself and called for the police. The murderer was gone long ago; but there lay his victim in the middle of the lane, incredibly mangled. The stick with which the deed had been done, although it was of some rare and very tough and heavy wood, had broken in the middle under the stress of this insensate cruelty; and one splintered half had rolled in the neighbouring gutter—the other, without doubt, had been carried away by the murderer. A purse and gold watch were found upon the victim: but no cards or papers, except a sealed and stamped envelope, which he had been probably carrying to the post, and which bore the name and address of Mr. Utterson.

This was brought to the lawyer the next morning, before he was out of bed; and he had no sooner seen it, and been told the circumstances, than he shot out a solemn lip. "I shall say nothing till I have seen the body," said he; "this may be very serious. Have the kindness to wait while I dress." And with the same grave countenance he hurried through his breakfast and drove to the police station, whither the body had been carried. As soon as he came into the cell, he nodded.

"Yes," said he, "I recognise him. I am sorry to say that this is Sir Danvers Carew."

"Good God, sir," exclaimed the officer, "is it possible?" And the next moment his eye lighted up with professional ambition. "This will make a deal of noise," he said. "And perhaps you can help us to the man." And he briefly narrated what the maid had seen, and showed the broken stick.

Mr. Utterson had already quailed at the name of Hyde; but when the stick was laid before him, he could doubt no longer; broken and battered as it was, he recognised it for one that he had himself presented many years before to Henry Jekyll.

"Is this Mr. Hyde a person of small stature?" he inquired.

"Particularly small and particularly wicked-looking, is what the maid calls him," said the officer.

Mr. Utterson reflected; and then, raising his head, "If you will come with me in my cab," he said, "I think I can take you to his house."

It was by this time about nine in the morning, and the first fog of the season. A great chocolate-coloured pall lowered over heaven, but the wind was continually charging and routing these embattled vapours; so that as

the cab crawled from street to street, Mr. Utterson beheld a marvelous number of degrees and hues of twilight; for here it would be dark like the backend of
evening; and there would be a glow of a rich, lurid brown,
like the light of some strange conflagration; and here, for
a moment, the fog would be quite broken up, and a haggard shaft of daylight would glance in between the swirling wreaths. The dismal quarter of Soho seen under
these changing glimpses, with its muddy ways, and slatternly passengers, and its lamps, which had never been
extinguished or had been kindled afresh to combat this
mournful reinvasion of darkness, seemed, in the lawyer's
eyes, like a district of some city in a nightmare. The
thoughts of his mind, besides, were of the gloomiest dye;
and when he glanced at the companion of his drive, he
was conscious of some touch of that terror of the law and
the law's officers, which may at times assail the most
honest.

As the cab drew up before the address indicated, the
fog lifted a little and showed him a dingy street, a gin
palace, a low French eating house, a shop for the retail of
penny numbers and twopenny salads, many ragged children huddled in the doorways, and many women of
many different nationalities passing out, key in hand, to
have a morning glass; and the next moment the fog set-
tled down again upon that part, as brown as umber, and
cut him off from his blackguardly surroundings. This was
the home of Henry Jekyll's favourite; of a man who was
heir to a quarter of a million sterling.

An ivory-faced and silvery-haired old woman opened
the door. She had an evil face, smoother by hypocrisy:
but her manners were excellent. Yes, she said, this was
Mr. Hyde's, but he was not at home; he had been in that
night very late, but he had gone away again in less than
an hour; there was nothing strange in that; his habits

were very irregular, and he was often absent; for instance, it was nearly two months since she had seen him till yesterday.

"Very well, then, we wish to see his room," said the lawyer; and when the woman began to declare it was impossible, "I had better tell you who this person is," he added. "This is Inspector Newcomen of Scotland Yard."

A flash of odious joy appeared upon the woman's face. "Ah!" said she, "he is in trouble! What has he done?"

Mr. Utterson and the inspector exchanged glances. "He don't seem a very popular character," observed the latter. "And now, my good woman, just let me and this gentleman have a look about us."

In the whole extent of the house, which but for the old woman remained otherwise empty, Mr. Hyde had only used a couple of rooms; but these were furnished with luxury and good taste. A closet was filled with wine; the plate was of silver, and napery elegant; a good picture hung upon the walls, a gift (as Utterson supposed) from Henry Jekyll, who was much of a connoisseur; and the carpets were of many plies and agreeable in colour. At this moment, however, the rooms bore every mark of having been recently and hurriedly ransacked; clothes lay about the floor, with their pockets inside out; lockfast drawers stood open; and on the hearth there lay a pile of grey ashes, as though many papers had been burned. From these embers the inspector disinterred the butt end of a green cheque book, which had resisted the action of the fire; the other half of the stick was found behind the door; and as this clinched his suspicions, the officer declared himself delighted. A visit to the bank, where several thousand pounds were found to be lying to the murderer's credit, completed his gratification.

"You may depend upon it, sir," he told Mr. Utterson:

"I have him in my hand. He must have lost his head, or he never would have left the stick or, above all, burned the cheque book. Why, money's life to the man. We have nothing to do but wait for him at the bank, and get out the handbills."

This last, however, was not so easy of accomplishment; for Mr. Hyde had numbered few familiars—even the master of the servant maid had only seen him twice; his family could nowhere be traced; he had never been photographed; and the few who could describe him differed widely, as common observers will. Only on one point were they agreed; and that was the haunting sense of unexpressed deformity with which the fugitive impressed his beholders.

INCIDENT OF THE LETTER

It was late in the afternoon, when Mr. Utterson found his way to Dr. Jekyll's door, where he was at once admitted by Poole, and carried down by the kitchen offices and across a yard which had once been a garden, to the building which was indifferently known as the laboratory or dissecting rooms. The doctor had bought the house from the heirs of a celebrated surgeon; and his own tastes being rather chemical than anatomical, had changed the destination of the block at the bottom of the garden. It was the first time that the lawyer had been received in that part of his friend's quarters; and he eyed the dingy, windowless structure with curiosity, and gazed round with a distasteful sense of strangeness as he crossed the theatre, once crowded with eager students and now lying gaunt and silent, the tables laden with chemical apparatus, the floor strewn with crates and littered with packing straw, and the light falling dimly through the foggy cupola. At the further end, a flight of stairs mounted to a door covered with red baize; and through this, Mr. Utterson was at last received into the doctor's cabinet. It was a large room fitted round with glass presses, furnished, among other things, with a cheval-glass and a business table, and looking out upon the court by three dusty windows barred with iron. The fire burned in the grate; a lamp was set lighted on the chimney shelf, for even in the houses the fog began to lie thickly; and there, close up to the warmth, sat Dr. Jekyll, looking deathly sick. He did not rise to meet his visitor, but held out a cold hand and bade him welcome in a changed voice.

"And now," said Mr. Utterson, as soon as Poole had left them, "you have heard the news?"

The doctor shuddered. "They were crying it in the square," he said. "I heard them in my dining-room."

"One word," said the lawyer. "Carew was my client, but so are you, and I want to know what I am doing. You have not been mad enough to hide this fellow?"

"Utterson, I swear to God," cried the doctor, "I swear to God I will never set eyes on him again. I bind my honour to you that I am done with him in this world. It is all at an end. And indeed he does not want my help; you do not know him as I do; he is safe, he is quite safe; mark my words, he will never more be heard of."

The lawyer listened gloomily; he did not like his friend's feverish manner. "You seem pretty sure of him," said he; "and for your sake, I hope you may be right. If it came to a trial, your name might appear."

"I am quite sure of him," replied Jekyll; "I have grounds for certainty that I cannot share with anyone. But there is one thing on which you may advise me. I have—I have received a letter; and I am at a loss whether I should show it to the police. I should like to leave it in your hands, Utterson; you would judge wisely, I am sure; I have so great a trust in you."

"You fear, I suppose, that it might lead to his detection?" asked the lawyer.

"No," said the other. "I cannot say that I care what becomes of Hyde; I am quite done with him. I was thinking of my own character, which this hateful business has rather exposed."

Utterson ruminated awhile; he was surprised at his friend's selfishness, and yet relieved by it. "Well," said he, at last, "let me see the letter."

The letter was written in an odd, upright hand and signed "Edward Hyde": and it signified, briefly enough, that the writer's benefactor, Dr. Jekyll, whom he had long so unworthily repaid for a thousand generosities, need labour under no alarm for his safety, as he had means of escape on which he placed a sure dependence. The lawyer liked this letter well enough; it put a better colour on the intimacy than he had looked for; and he blamed himself for some of his past suspicions.

"Have you the envelope?" he asked.

"I burned it," replied Jekyll, "before I thought what I was about. But it bore no postmark. The note was handed in."

"Shall I keep this and sleep upon it?" asked Utterson.

"I wish you to judge for me entirely," was the reply. "I have lost confidence in myself."

"Well, I shall consider," returned the lawyer. "And now one word more: it was Hyde who dictated the terms in your will about that disappearance?"

The doctor seemed seized with a qualm of faintness; he shut his mouth tight and nodded.

"I knew it," said Utterson. "He meant to murder you. You had a fine escape."

"I have had what is far more to the purpose," returned the doctor solemnly: "I have had a lesson—O God, Utterson, what a lesson I have had!" And he covered his face for a moment with his hands.

On his way out, the lawyer stopped and had a word or two with Poole. "By the bye," said he, "there was a letter handed in to-day: what was the messenger like?" But

Poole was positive nothing had come except by post; "and only circulars by that," he added.

This news sent off the visitor with his fears renewed. Plainly the letter had come by the laboratory door; possibly, indeed, it had been written in the cabinet; and if that were so, it must be differently judged, and handled with the more caution. The newsboys, as he went, were crying themselves hoarse along the footways: "Special edition. Shocking murder of an M.P." That was the funeral oration of one friend and client; and he could not help a certain apprehension lest the good name of another should be sucked down in the eddy of the scandal. It was, at least, a ticklish decision that he had to make; and self-reliant as he was by habit, he began to cherish a longing for advice. It was not to be had directly; but perhaps, he thought, it might be fished for.

Presently after, he sat on one side of his own hearth, with Mr. Guest, his head clerk, upon the other, and midway between, at a nicely calculated distance from the fire, a bottle of a particular old wine that had long dwelt unsunned in the foundations of his house. The fog still slept on the wing above the drowned city, where the lamps glimmered like carbuncles; and through the muffle and smother of these fallen clouds, the procession of the town's life was still rolling in through the great arteries with a sound as of a mighty wind. But the room was gay with firelight. In the bottle the acids were long ago resolved; the imperial dye had softened with time, as the colour grows richer in stained windows; and the glow of hot autumn afternoons on hillside vineyards was ready to be set free and to disperse the fogs of London. Insensibly the lawyer melted. There was no man from whom he kept fewer secrets than Mr. Guest; and he was not always sure that he kept as many as he meant. Guest had often been on business to the doctor's; he knew Poole;

he could scarce have failed to hear of Mr. Hyde's familiarity about the house; he might draw conclusions: was it not as well, then, that he should see a letter which put that mystery to rights? and above all since Guest, being a great student and critic of handwriting, would consider the step natural and obliging? The clerk, besides, was a man of counsel; he could scarce read so strange a document without dropping a remark; and by that remark Mr. Utterson might shape his future course.

"This is a sad business about Sir Danvers," he said.

"Yes, sir, indeed. It has elicited a great deal of public feeling," returned Guest. "The man, of course, was mad."

"I should like to hear your views on that," replied Utterson. "I have a document here in his handwriting; it is between ourselves, for I scarce know what to do about it; it is an ugly business at the best. But there it is; quite in your way: a murderer's autograph."

Guest's eyes brightened, and he sat down at once and studied it with passion. "No sir," he said: "not mad; but it is an odd hand."

"And by all accounts a very odd writer," added the lawyer.

Just then the servant entered with a note.

"Is that from Dr. Jekyll, sir?" inquired the clerk. "I thought I knew the writing. Anything private, Mr. Utterson?"

"Only an invitation to dinner. Why? Do you want to see it?"

"One moment. I thank you, sir"; and the clerk laid the two sheets of paper alongside and sedulously compared their contents. "Thank you, sir," he said at last, returning both; "it's a very interesting autograph."

There was a pause, during which Mr. Utterson struggled with himself. "Why did you compare them, Guest?" he inquired suddenly.

"Well, sir," returned the clerk, "there's a rather singular resemblance; the two hands are in many points identical: only differently sloped."

"Rather quaint," said Utterson.

"It is, as you say, rather quaint," returned Guest.

"I wouldn't speak of this note, you know," said the master.

"No, sir," said the clerk. "I understand."

But no sooner was Mr. Utterson alone that night, than he locked the note into his safe, where it reposed from that time forward. "What!" he thought. "Henry Jekyll forge for a murderer!" and his blood ran cold in his veins.

REMARKABLE INCIDENT
OF DR. LANYON

Time ran on; thousands of pounds were offered in reward, for the death of Sir Danvers was resented as a public injury; but Mr. Hyde had disappeared out of the ken of the police as though he had never existed. Much of his past was unearthed, indeed, and all disreputable: tales came out of the man's cruelty, at once so callous and violent; of his vile life, of his strange associates, of the hatred that seemed to have surrounded his career; but of his present whereabouts, not a whisper. From the time he had left the house in Soho on the morning of the murder, he was simply blotted out; and gradually, as time drew on, Mr. Utterson began to recover from the hotness of his alarm, and to grow more at quiet with himself. The death of Sir Danvers was, to his way of thinking, more than paid for by the disappearance of Mr. Hyde. Now that that evil influence had been withdrawn, a new life began for Dr. Jekyll. He came out of his seclusion, renewed relations with his friends, became once more their familiar guest and entertainer; and whilst he had always been known for charities, he was now no less distinguished for religion. He was busy, he was much in the open air, he did good; his face seemed to open and brighten, as if with an inward consciousness of service; and for more than two months, the doctor was at peace.

On the 8th of January Utterson had dined at the doctor's with a small party; Lanyon had been there; and the face of the host had looked from one to the other as in the old days when the trio were inseparable friends. On the 12th, and again on the 14th, the door was shut against the lawyer. "The doctor was confined to the house," Poole said, "and saw no one." On the 15th, he tried again, and was again refused; and having now been used for the last two months to see his friend almost daily, he found this return of solitude to weigh upon his spirits. The fifth night he had in Guest to dine with him; and the sixth he betook himself to Dr. Lanyon's.

There at least he was not denied admittance; but when he came in, he was shocked at the change which had taken place in the doctor's appearance. He had his death-warrant written legibly upon his face. The rosy man had grown pale; his flesh had fallen away; he was visibly balder and older; and yet it was not so much these tokens of a swift physical decay that arrested the lawyer's notice, as a look in the eye and quality of manner that seemed to testify to some deep-seated terror of the mind. It was unlikely that the doctor should fear death; and yet that was what Utterson was tempted to suspect. "Yes," he thought; "he is a doctor, he must know his own state and that his days are counted; and the knowledge is more than he can bear." And yet when Utterson remarked on his ill-looks, it was with an air of great firmness that Lanyon declared himself a doomed man.

"I have had a shock," he said, "and I shall never recover. It is a question of weeks. Well, life has been pleasant; I liked it; yes, sir, I used to like it. I sometimes think if we knew all, we should be more glad to get away."

"Jekyll is ill, too," observed Utterson. "Have you seen him?"

But Lanyon's face changed, and he held up a trembling hand. "I wish to see or hear no more of Dr. Jekyll," he said in a loud, unsteady voice. "I am quite done with that person; and I beg that you will spare me any allusion to one whom I regard as dead."

"Tut-tut," said Mr. Utterson; and then after a considerable pause, "Can't I do anything?" he inquired. "We are three very old friends, Lanyon; we shall not live to make others."

"Nothing can be done," returned Lanyon; "ask himself."

"He will not see me," said the lawyer.

"I am not surprised at that," was the reply. "Some day, Utterson, after I am dead, you may perhaps come to learn the right and wrong of this. I cannot tell you. And in the meantime, if you can sit and talk with me of other things, for God's sake, stay and do so; but if you cannot keep clear of this accursed topic, then in God's name, go, for I cannot bear it."

As soon as he got home, Utterson sat down and wrote to Jekyll, complaining of his exclusion from the house, and asking the cause of this unhappy break with Lanyon; and the next day brought him a long answer, often very pathetically worded, and sometimes darkly mysterious in drift. The quarrel with Lanyon was incurable. "I do not blame our old friend," Jekyll wrote, "but I share his view that we must never meet. I mean from henceforth to lead a life of extreme seclusion; you must not be surprised, nor must you doubt my friendship, if my door is often shut even to you. You must suffer me to go my own dark way. I have brought on myself a punishment and a danger that I cannot name. If I am the chief of sinners, I am the chief of sufferers also. I could not think that this

earth contained a place for sufferings and terrors so un-
manning; and you can do but one thing, Utterson, to
lighten this destiny, and that is to respect my silence."
Utterson was amazed; the dark influence of Hyde had
been withdrawn, the doctor had returned to his old tasks
and amities; a week ago, the prospect had smiled with
every promise of a cheerful and an honoured age; and
now in a moment, friendship, and peace of mind, and the
whole tenor of his life were wrecked. So great and un-
prepared a change pointed to madness; but in view of
Lanyon's manner and words, there must lie for it some
deeper ground.

A week afterwards Dr. Lanyon took to his bed, and in
something less than a fortnight he was dead. The night
after the funeral, at which he had been sadly affected,
Utterson locked the door of his business room, and sitting there by the light of a melancholy candle, drew out
and set before him an envelope addressed by the hand
and sealed with the seal of his dead friend. "PRIVATE: for
the hands of G.J. Utterson ALONE, and in case of his pre-
decease *to be destroyed unread*," so it was emphatically
superscribed; and the lawyer dreaded to behold the contents. "I have buried one friend to-day," he thought:
"what if this should cost me another?" And then he condemned the fear as a disloyalty, and broke the seal.
Within there was another enclosure, likewise sealed, and
marked upon the cover as "not to be opened till the
death or disappearance of Dr. Henry Jekyll." Utterson
could not trust his eyes. Yes, it was disappearance; here
again, as in the mad will which he had long ago restored
to its author, here again were the idea of a disappearance
and the name of Henry Jekyll bracketed. But in the will,
that idea had sprung from the sinister suggestion of the
man Hyde; it was set there with a purpose all too plain
and horrible. Written by the hand of Lanyon, what

should it mean? A great curiosity came on the trustee, to disregard the prohibition and dive at once to the bottom of these mysteries; but professional honour and faith to his dead friend were stringent obligations; and the packet slept in the inmost corner of his private safe.

It is one thing to mortify curiosity, another to conquer it; and it may be doubted if, from that day forth, Utterson desired the society of his surviving friend with the same eagerness. He thought of him kindly; but his thoughts were disquieted and fearful. He went to call indeed; but he was perhaps relieved to be denied admittance; perhaps, in his heart, he preferred to speak with Poole upon the doorstep and surrounded by the air and sounds of the open city, rather than to be admitted into that house of voluntary bondage, and to sit and speak with its inscrutable recluse. Poole had, indeed, no very pleasant news to communicate. The doctor, it appeared, now more than ever confined himself to the cabinet over the laboratory, where he would sometimes even sleep; he was out of spirits, he had grown very silent, he did not read; it seemed as if he had something on his mind. Utterson became so used to the unvarying character of these reports, that he fell off little by little in the frequency of his visits.

INCIDENT AT THE WINDOW

It chanced on Sunday, when Mr. Utterson was on his usual walk with Mr. Enfield, that their way lay once again through the by-street; and that when they came in front of the door, both stopped to gaze on it.

"Well," said Enfield, "that story's at an end at least. We shall never see more of Mr. Hyde."

"I hope not," said Utterson. "Did I ever tell you that I once saw him, and shared your feeling of repulsion?"

"It was impossible to do the one without the other," returned Enfield. "And by the way, what an ass you must have thought me, not to know that this was a back way to Dr. Jekyll's! It was partly your own fault that I found it out, even when I did."

"So you found it out, did you?" said Utterson. "But if that be so, we may step into the court and take a look at the windows. To tell you the truth, I am uneasy about poor Jekyll; and even outside, I feel as if the presence of a friend might do him good."

The court was very cool and a little damp, and full of premature twilight, although the sky, high up overhead, was still bright with sunset. The middle one of the three windows was half-way open; and sitting close beside it, taking the air with an infinite sadness of mien, like some disconsolate prisoner, Utterson saw Dr. Jekyll.

"What! Jekyll!" he cried, "I trust you are better."

"I am very low, Utterson," replied the doctor drearily, "very low. It will not last long, thank God."

"You stay too much indoors," said the lawyer. "You should be out, whipping up the circulation like Mr. Enfield and me. (This is my cousin—Mr. Enfield—Dr. Jekyll.) Come now; get your hat and take a quick turn with us."

"You are very good," sighed the other. "I should like to very much; but no, no, no, it is quite impossible; I dare not. But indeed, Utterson, I am very glad to see you; this is really a great pleasure; I would ask you and Mr. Enfield up, but the place is really not fit."

"Why, then," said the lawyer, good-naturedly, "the best thing we can do is to stay down here and speak with you from where we are."

"That is just what I was about to venture to propose," returned the doctor with a smile. But the words were hardly uttered, before the smile was struck out of his face and succeeded by an expression of such abject terror and despair, as froze the very blood of the two gentlemen below. They saw it but for a glimpse, for the window was instantly thrust down; but that glimpse had been sufficient, and they turned and left the court without a word. In silence, too, they traversed the by-street; and it was not until they had come into a neighbouring thoroughfare, where even upon a Sunday there were still some stirrings of life, that Mr. Utterson at last turned and looked at his companion. They were both pale; and there was an answering horror in their eyes.

"God forgive us, God forgive us," said Mr. Utterson.

But Mr. Enfield only nodded his head very seriously, and walked on once more in silence.

THE LAST NIGHT

Mr. Utterson was sitting by his fireside one evening after dinner, when he was surprised to receive a visit from Poole.

"Bless me, Poole, what brings you here?" he cried; and then taking a second look at him, "What ails you?" he added; "is the doctor ill?"

"Mr. Utterson," said the man, "there is something wrong."

"Take a seat, and here is a glass of wine for you," said the lawyer. "Now, take your time, and tell me plainly what you want."

"You know the doctor's ways, sir," replied Poole, "and how he shuts himself up. Well, he's shut up again in the cabinet; and I don't like it, sir—I wish I may die if I like it. Mr. Utterson, sir, I'm afraid."

"Now, my good man," said the lawyer, "be explicit. What are you afraid of?"

"I've been afraid for about a week," returned Poole, doggedly disregarding the question, "and I can bear it no more."

The man's appearance amply bore out his words; his manner was altered for the worse; and except for the moment when he had first announced his terror, he had not once looked the lawyer in the face. Even now, he sat with the glass of wine untasted on his knee, and his eyes directed to a corner of the floor. "I can bear it no more," he repeated.

"Come," said the lawyer, "I see you have some good reason, Poole; I see there is something seriously amiss. Try to tell me what it is."

"I think there's been foul play," said Poole, hoarsely.

"Foul play!" cried the lawyer, a good deal frightened and rather inclined to be irritated in consequence. "What foul play! What does the man mean?"

"I daren't say, sir," was the answer; "but will you come along with me and see for yourself?"

Mr. Utterson's only answer was to rise and get his hat and greatcoat; but he observed with wonder the greatness of the relief that appeared upon the butler's face, and perhaps with no less, that the wine was still untasted when he set it down to follow.

It was a wild, cold, seasonable night of March, with a pale moon, lying on her back as though the wind had tilted her, and flying wrack of the most diaphanous and lawny texture. The wind made talking difficult, and flecked the blood into the face. It seemed to have swept the streets unusually bare of passengers, besides; for Mr. Utterson thought he had never seen that part of London so deserted. He could have wished it otherwise; never in his life had he been conscious of so sharp a wish to see and touch his fellow-creatures; for struggle as he might, there was borne in upon his mind a crushing anticipation of calamity. The square, when they got there, was full of wind and dust, and the thin trees in the garden were lashing themselves along the railing. Poole, who had kept all the way a pace or two ahead, now pulled up in the middle of the pavement, and in spite of the biting weather, took off his hat and mopped his brow with a red pocket handkerchief. But for all the hurry of his coming, these were not the dews of exertion that he wiped away, but the moisture of some strangling anguish; for his face was white and his voice, when he spoke, harsh and broken.

"Well, sir," he said, "here we are, and God grant there be nothing wrong."

"Amen, Poole," said the lawyer.

Thereupon the servant knocked in a very guarded manner; the door was opened on the chain; and a voice asked from within, "Is that you, Poole?"

"It's all right," said Poole. "Open the door."

The hall, when they entered it, was brightly lighted up; the fire was built high; and about the hearth the whole of the servants, men and women, stood huddled together like a flock of sheep. At the sight of Mr. Utterson, the housemaid broke into hysterical whimpering; and the cook, crying out, "Bless God! it's Mr. Utterson," ran forward as if to take him in her arms.

"What, what? Are you all here?" said the lawyer peevishly. "Very irregular, very unseemly; your master would be far from pleased."

"They're all afraid," said Poole.

Blank silence followed, no one protesting; only the maid lifted her voice and now wept loudly.

"Hold your tongue!" Poole said to her, with a ferocity of accent that testified to his own jangled nerves; and indeed, when the girl had so suddenly raised the note of her lamentation, they had all started and turned towards the inner door with faces of dreadful expectation. "And now," continued the butler, addressing the knife-boy, "reach me a candle, and we'll get this through hands at once." And then he begged Mr. Utterson to follow him, and led the way to the back garden.

"Now, sir," said he, "you come as gently as you can. I

want you to hear, and I don't want you to be heard. And see here, sir, if by any chance he was to ask you in, don't go."

Mr. Utterson's nerves, at this unlooked-for termination, gave a jerk that nearly threw him from balance; but he recollected his courage and followed the butler into the laboratory building through the surgical theatre, with its lumber of crates and bottles, to the foot of the stair. Here Poole motioned him to stand on one side and listen; while he himself, setting down the candle and making a great and obvious call on his resolution, mounted the steps and knocked with a somewhat uncertain hand on the red baize of the cabinet door.

"Mr. Utterson, sir, asking to see you," he called; and even as he did so, once more violently signed to the lawyer to give ear.

A voice answered from within: "Tell him I cannot see anyone," it said complainingly.

"Thank you, sir," said Poole, with a note of something like triumph in his voice; and taking up his candle, he led Mr. Utterson back across the yard and into the great kitchen, where the fire was out and the beetles were leaping on the floor.

"Sir," he said, looking Mr. Utterson in the eyes, "was that my master's voice?"

"It seems much changed," replied the lawyer, very pale, but giving look for look.

"Changed? Well, yes, I think so," said the butler. "Have I been twenty years in this man's house, to be deceived about his voice? No, sir; master's made away with; he was made away with eight days ago, when we heard him cry out upon the name of God; and *who's* in there instead of him, and *why* it stays there, is a thing that cries to Heaven, Mr. Utterson!"

"This is a very strange tale, Poole; this is rather a wild

tale, my man," said Mr. Utterson, biting his finger. "Suppose it were as you suppose, supposing Dr. Jekyll to have been—well, murdered, what could induce the murderer to stay? That won't hold water; it doesn't commend itself to reason."

"Well, Mr. Utterson, you are a hard man to satisfy, but I'll do it yet," said Poole. "All this last week (you must know) him, or it, whatever it is that lives in that cabinet, has been crying night and day for some sort of medicine and cannot get it to his mind. It was sometimes his way— the master's, that is—to write his orders on a sheet of paper and throw it on the stair. We've had nothing else this week back; nothing but papers, and a closed door, and the very meals left there to be smuggled in when nobody was looking. Well, sir, every day, ay, and twice and thrice in the same day, there have been orders and complaints, and I have been sent flying to all the wholesale chemists in town. Every time I brought the stuff back, there would be another paper telling me to return it, because it was not pure, and another order to a different firm. This drug is wanted bitter bad, sir, whatever for."

"Have you any of these papers?" asked Mr. Utterson.

Poole felt in his pocket and handed out a crumpled note, which the lawyer, bending nearer to the candle, carefully examined. Its contents ran thus: "Dr. Jekyll presents his compliments to Messrs. Maw. He assures them that their last sample is impure and quite useless for his present purpose. In the year 18—, Dr. J. purchased a somewhat large quantity from Messrs. M. He now begs them to search with most sedulous care, and should any of the same quality be left, to forward it to him at once. Expense is no consideration. The importance of this to Dr. J. can hardly be exaggerated." So far the letter had run composedly enough, but here with a sudden splutter of the pen, the writer's emotion had broken loose. "For God's sake," he added, "find me some of the old."

"This is a strange note," said Mr. Utterson; and then sharply, "How do you come to have it open?"

"The man at Maw's was main angry, sir, and he threw it back to me like so much dirt," returned Poole.

"This is unquestionably the doctor's hand, do you know?" resumed the lawyer.

"I thought it looked like it," said the servant rather sulkily; and then, with another voice, "But what matters hand of write?" he said. "I've seen him!"

"Seen him?" repeated Mr. Utterson. "Well?"

"That's it!" said Poole. "It was this way. I came suddenly into the theatre from the garden. It seems he had slipped out to look for this drug or whatever it is; for the cabinet door was open, and there he was at the far end of the room digging among the crates. He looked up when I came in, gave a kind of cry, and whipped upstairs into the cabinet. It was but for one minute that I saw him, but the hair stood upon my head like quills. Sir, if that was my master, why had he a mask upon his face? If it was my master, why did he cry out like a rat, and run from me? I have served long enough. And then . . ." The man paused and passed his hand over his face.

"These are all very strange circumstances," said Mr. Utterson, "but I think I begin to see daylight. Your master, Poole, is plainly seized with one of those maladies that both torture and deform the sufferer; hence, for aught I know, the alteration of his voice; hence the mask and the avoidance of his friends; hence his eagerness to find this drug, by means of which the poor soul retains some hope of ultimate recovery—God grant that he be not deceived! There is my explanation; it is sad enough, Poole, ay, and appalling to consider; but it is plain and natural, hangs well together, and delivers us from all exorbitant alarms."

"Sir," said the butler, turning to a sort of mottled pallor, "that thing was not my master, and there's the truth. My master"—here he looked round him and began to whisper—"is a tall, fine build of a man, and this was more of a dwarf." Utterson attempted to protest. "Oh, sir," cried Poole, "do you think I do not know my master after twenty years? Do you think I do not know where his head comes to in the cabinet door, where I saw him every morning of my life? No, sir, that thing in the mask was never Dr. Jekyll—God knows what it was, but it was never Dr. Jekyll; and it is the belief of my heart that there was murder done."

"Poole," replied the lawyer, "if you say that, it will become my duty to make certain. Much as I desire to spare your master's feelings, much as I am puzzled by this note which seems to prove him to be still alive, I shall consider it my duty to break in that door."

"Ah, Mr. Utterson, that's talking!" cried the butler.

"And now comes the second question," resumed Utterson: "Who is going to do it?"

"Why, you and me, sir," was the undaunted reply.

"That's very well said," returned the lawyer; "and whatever comes of it, I shall make it my business to see you are no loser."

"There is an axe in the theatre," continued Poole; "and you might take the kitchen poker for yourself."

The lawyer took that rude but weighty instrument into his hand, and balanced it. "Do you know, Poole," he said, looking up, "that you and I are about to place ourselves in a position of some peril?"

"You may say so, sir, indeed," returned the butler.

"It is well, then, that we should be frank," said the other. "We both think more than we have said; let us make a clean breast. This masked figure that you saw, did you recognize it?"

"Well, sir, it went so quick, and the creature was so doubled up, that I could hardly swear to that," was the answer. "But if you mean, was it Mr. Hyde?—why, yes, I think it was! You see, it was much of the same bigness; and it had the same quick, light way with it; and then who else could have got in by the laboratory door? You have not forgot, sir, that at the time of the murder he had still the key with him? But that's not all. I don't know, Mr. Utterson, if you ever met this Mr. Hyde?"

"Yes," said the lawyer, "I once spoke with him."

"Then you must know as well as the rest of us that there was something queer about that gentleman—something that gave a man a turn—I don't know rightly how to say it, sir, beyond this: that you felt in your marrow kind of cold and thin."

"I own I felt something of what you describe," said Mr. Utterson.

"Quite so, sir," returned Poole. "Well, when that masked thing like a monkey jumped from among the chemicals and whipped into the cabinet, it went down my spine like ice. O, I know it's not evidence, Mr. Utterson; I'm book-learned enough for that; but a man has his feelings, and I give you my bible-word it was Mr. Hyde!"

"Ay, ay," said the lawyer. "My fears incline to the same point. Evil, I fear, founded—evil was sure to come—of that connection. Ay truly, I believe you; I believe poor Harry is killed; and I believe his murderer (for what purpose, God alone can tell) is still lurking in his victim's room. Well, let our name be vengeance. Call Bradshaw."

The footman came at the summons, very white and nervous.

"Put yourself together, Bradshaw," said the lawyer. "This suspense, I know, is telling upon all of you; but it is now our intention to make an end of it. Poole, here, and I are going to force our way into the cabinet. If all is well, my shoulders are broad enough to bear the blame. Meanwhile, lest anything should really be amiss, or any malefactor seek to escape by the back, you and the boy must go round the corner with a pair of good sticks and take your post at the laboratory door. We give you ten minutes, to get to your stations."

As Bradshaw left, the lawyer looked at his watch. "And now, Poole, let us get to ours," he said; and taking the poker under his arm, led the way into the yard. The scud had banked over the moon, and it was now quite dark. The wind, which only broke in puffs and draughts into that deep well of building, tossed the light of the candle to and fro about their steps, until they came into the shelter of the theatre, where they sat down silently to wait. London hummed solemnly all around; but nearer at hand, the stillness was only broken by the sounds of a footfall moving to and fro along the cabinet floor.

"So it will walk all day, sir," whispered Poole; "ay, and the better part of the night. Only when a new sample comes from the chemist, there's a bit of a break. Ah, it's an ill conscience that's such an enemy to rest! Ah, sir, there's blood foully shed in every step of it! But hark again, a little closer—put your heart in your ears, Mr. Utterson, and tell me, is that the doctor's foot?"

The steps fell lightly and oddly, with a certain swing, for all they went so slowly; it was different indeed from the heavy creaking tread of Henry Jekyll. Utterson sighed. "Is there never anything else?" he asked.

Poole nodded. "Once," he said. "Once I heard it weeping!"

"Weeping? how that?" said the lawyer, conscious of a sudden chill of horror.

"Weeping like a woman or a lost soul," said the butler.

"I came away with that upon my heart, that I could have wept too."

But now the ten minutes drew to an end. Poole disinterred the axe from under a stack of packing straw; the candle was set upon the nearest table to light them to the attack; and they drew near with bated breath to where that patient foot was still going up and down, up and down, in the quiet of the night. "Jekyll," cried Utterson, with a loud voice, "I demand to see you." He paused a moment, but there came no reply. "I give you fair warning, our suspicions are aroused, and I must and shall see you," he resumed; "if not by fair means, then by foul—if not of your consent, then by brute force!"

"Utterson," said the voice, "for God's sake, have mercy!"

"Ah, that's not Jekyll's voice—it's Hyde's!" cried Utterson. "Down with the door, Poole!"

Poole swung the axe over his shoulder; the blow shook the building, and the red baize door leaped against the lock and hinges. A dismal screech, as of mere animal terror, rang from the cabinet. Up went the axe again, and again the panels crashed and the frame bounded; four times the blow fell; but the wood was tough and the fittings were of excellent workmanship; and it was not until the fifth, that the lock burst and the wreck of the door fell inwards on the carpet.

The besiegers, appalled by their own riot and the stillness that had succeeded, stood back a little and peered in. There lay the cabinet before their eyes in the quiet lamplight, a good fire glowing and chattering on the hearth, the kettle singing its thin strain, a drawer or two open, papers neatly set forth on the business table, and nearer the fire, the things laid out for tea; the quietest room, you would have said, and, for the glazed presses full of chemicals, the most commonplace that night in London.

Right in the midst there lay the body of a man sorely

contorted and still twitching. They drew near on tiptoe, turned it on its back and beheld the face of Edward Hyde. He was dressed in clothes far too large for him, clothes of the doctor's bigness; the cords of his face still moved with a semblance of life, but life was quite gone: and by the crushed phial in the hand and the strong smell of kernels that hung upon the air, Utterson knew that he was looking on the body of a self-destroyer.

"We have come too late," he said sternly, "whether to save or punish. Hyde is gone to his account; and it only remains for us to find the body of your master."

The far greater proportion of the building was occupied by the theatre, which filled almost the whole ground storey and was lighted from above, and by the cabinet, which formed an upper storey at one end and looked upon a court. A corridor joined the theatre to the door on the by-street; and with this the cabinet communicated separately by a second flight of stairs. There were besides a few dark closets and a spacious cellar. All these they now thoroughly examined. Each closet needed but a glance, for all were empty, and all, by the dust that fell from their doors, had stood long unopened. The cellar, indeed, was filled with crazy lumber, mostly dating from the times of the surgeon who was Jekyll's predecessor; but even as they opened the door they were advertised of the uselessness of further search, by the fall of a perfect mat of cobweb which had for years sealed up the entrance. Nowhere was there any trace of Henry Jekyll, dead or alive.

Poole stamped on the flags of the corridor. "He must be buried here," he said, hearkening to the sound.

"Or he may have fled," said Utterson, and he turned to examine the door in the by-street. It was locked; and lying near by on the flags, they found the key, already stained with rust.

"This does not look like use," observed the lawyer.

"Use!" echoed Poole. "Do you not see, sir, it is broken? much as if a man had stamped on it."

"Ay," continued Utterson, "and the fractures, too, are rusty." The two men looked at each other with a scare. "This is beyond me, Poole," said the lawyer. "Let us go back to the cabinet."

They mounted the stair in silence, and still with an occasional awestruck glance at the dead body, proceeded more thoroughly to examine the contents of the cabinet. At one table, there were traces of chemical work, various measured heaps of some white salt being laid on glass saucers, as though for an experiment in which the unhappy man had been prevented.

"That is the same drug that I was always bringing him," said Poole; and even as he spoke, the kettle with a startling noise boiled over.

This brought them to the fireside, where the easy-chair was drawn cosily up, and the tea things stood ready to the sitter's elbow, the very sugar in the cup. There were several books on a shelf; one lay beside the tea things open, and Utterson was amazed to find it a copy of a pious work, for which Jekyll had several times expressed a great esteem, annotated, in his own hand, with startling blasphemies.

Next, in the course of their review of the chamber, the searchers came to the cheval-glass, into whose depths they looked with an involuntary horror. But it was so turned as to show them nothing but the rosy glow playing on the roof, the fire sparkling in a hundred repetitions along the glazed front of the presses, and their own pale and fearful countenances stooping to look in.

"This glass has seen some strange things, sir," whispered Poole.

"And surely none stranger than itself," echoed the lawyer in the same tones. "For what did Jekyll"—he caught himself up at the word with a start, and then conquering the weakness—"what could Jekyll want with it?" he said.

"You may say that!" said Poole.

Next they turned to the business table. On the desk, among the neat array of papers, a large envelope was uppermost, and bore, in the doctor's hand, the name of Mr. Utterson. The lawyer unsealed it, and several enclosures fell to the floor. The first was a will, drawn in the same eccentric terms as the one which he had returned six months before, to serve as a testament in case of death and as a deed of gift in case of disappearance; but in place of the name of Edward Hyde, the lawyer, with indescribable amazement, read the name of Gabriel John Utterson. He looked at Poole, and then back at the paper, and last of all at the dead malefactor stretched upon the carpet.

"My head goes round," he said. "He has been all these days in possession; he had no cause to like me; he must have raged to see himself displaced; and he has not destroyed this document."

He caught up the next paper; it was a brief note in the doctor's hand and dated at the top. "O Poole!" the lawyer cried, "he was alive and here this day. He cannot have been disposed of in so short a space; he must be still alive, he must have fled! And then, why fled! and how? and in that case, can we venture to declare this suicide? O, we must be careful. I foresee that we may yet involve your master in some dire catastrophe."

"Why don't you read it, sir?" asked Poole.

"Because I fear," replied the lawyer solemnly. "God grant I have no cause for it!" And with that he brought the paper to his eyes and read as follows:

My dear Utterson, — When this shall fall into your hands, I shall have disappeared, under what circumstances I have not the penetration to foresee, but my instinct and all the circumstances of my nameless situation tell me that the end is sure and must be early. Go then, and first read the narrative which Lanyon warned me he was to place in your hands; and if you care to hear more, turn to the confession of

Your unworthy and unhappy friend,

HENRY JEKYLL.

"There was a third enclosure?" asked Utterson.

"Here, sir," said Poole, and gave into his hands a considerable packet sealed in several places.

The lawyer put it in his pocket. "I would say nothing of this paper. If your master has fled or is dead, we may at least save his credit. It is now ten; I must go home and read these documents in quiet; but I shall be back before midnight, when we shall send for the police."

They went out, locking the door of the theatre behind them; and Utterson, once more leaving the servants gathered about the fire in the hall, trudged back to his office to read the two narratives in which this mystery was now to be explained.

Dr. Lanyon's Narrative

On the ninth of January, now four days ago, I received by the evening delivery a registered envelope, addressed in the hand of my colleague and old school companion, Henry Jekyll. I was a good deal surprised by this; for we were by no means in the habit of correspondence; I had seen the man, dined with him, indeed, the night before; and I could imagine nothing in our intercourse that should justify formality of registration. The contents increased my wonder; for this is how the letter ran:

> *10th December, 18—.*
>
> *Dear Lanyon,—You are one of my oldest friends; and although we may have differed at times on scientific questions, I cannot remember, at least on my side, any break in our affection. There was never a day when, if you had said to me, "Jekyll, my life, my honour, my reason, depend upon you," I would not have sacrificed my left hand to help you. Lanyon, my life, my honour, my reason, are all at your mercy; if you fail me to-night, I am lost. You might suppose, after this preface, that I am going to ask you for something dishonourable to grant. Judge for yourself.*

*I want you to postpone all other engagements for
to-night—ay, even if you were summoned to the
bedside of an emperor; to take a cab, unless your
carriage should be actually at the door; and with this
letter in your hand for consultation, to drive straight
to my house. Poole, my butler, has his orders; you
will find him waiting your arrival with a locksmith.
The door of my cabinet is then to be forced: and you
are to go in alone; to open the glazed press (letter E)
on the left hand, breaking the lock if it be shut; and
to draw out,* with all its contents as they stand, *the
fourth drawer from the top or (which is the same
thing) the third from the bottom. In my extreme distress of mind, I have a morbid fear of misdirecting
you; but even if I am in error, you may know the
right drawer by its contents: some powders, a phial
and a paper book. This drawer I beg of you to carry
back with you to Cavendish Square exactly as it
stands.*

*That is the first part of the service: now for the
second. You should be back, if you set out at once
on the receipt of this, long before midnight; but I will
leave you that amount of margin, not only in the
fear of one of those obstacles that can neither be
prevented nor foreseen, but because an hour when
your servants are in bed is to be preferred for what
will then remain to do. At midnight, then, I have to
ask you to be alone in your consulting room, to admit with your own hand into the house a man who
will present himself in my name, and to place in his
hands the drawer that you will have brought with
you from my cabinet. Then you will have played
your part and earned my gratitude completely. Five
minutes afterwards, if you insist upon an explanation, you will have understood that these arrange-*

ments are of capital importance; and that by the neglect of one of them, fantastic as they must appear, you might have charged your conscience with my death or the shipwreck of my reason.

Confident as I am that you will not trifle with this appeal, my heart sinks and my hand trembles at the bare thought of such a possibility. Think of me at this hour, in a strange place, labouring under a blackness of distress that no fancy can exaggerate, and yet well aware that, if you will but punctually serve me, my troubles will roll away like a story that is told. Serve me, my dear Lanyon, and save

Your friend,

H. J.

P.S.—I had already sealed this up when a fresh terror struck upon my soul. It is possible that the post-office may fail me, and this letter not come into your hands until tomorrow morning. In that case, dear Lanyon, do my errand when it shall be most convenient for you in the course of the day; and once more expect my messenger at midnight. It may then already be too late; and if that night passes without event, you will know that you have seen the last of Henry Jekyll.

Upon the reading of this letter, I made sure my colleague was insane; but till that was proved beyond the possibility of doubt, I felt bound to do as he requested. The less I understood of this farrago, the less I was in a position to judge of its importance; and an appeal so worded could not be set aside without a grave responsibility. I rose accordingly from table, got into a hansom, and drove straight to Jekyll's house. The butler was awaiting my arrival; he had received by the same post as

mine a registered letter of instruction, and had sent at
once for a locksmith and a carpenter. The tradesmen
came while we were yet speaking; and we moved in a
body to old Dr. Denman's surgical theatre, from which
(as you are doubtless aware) Jekyll's private cabinet is
most conveniently entered. The door was very strong,
the lock excellent; the carpenter avowed he would have
great trouble and have to do much damage, if force were
to be used; and the locksmith was near despair. But this
last was a handy fellow, and after two hours' work, the
door stood open. The press marked E was unlocked; and
I took out the drawer, had it filled up with straw and tied
in a sheet, and returned with it to Cavendish Square.

Here I proceeded to examine its contents. The powders were neatly enough made up, but not with the
nicety of the dispensing chemist; so that it was plain they
were of Jekyll's private manufacture: and when I opened
one of the wrappers I found what seemed to me a simple
crystalline salt of a white colour. The phial, to which I
next turned my attention, might have been about half
full of a blood-red liquor, which was highly pungent to
the sense of smell and seemed to me to contain phos-
phorus and some volatile ether. At the other ingredients
I could make no guess. The book was an ordinary version
book and contained little but a series of dates. These covered a period of many years, but I observed that the entries ceased nearly a year ago and quite abruptly. Here
and there a brief remark was appended to a date, usually
no more than a single word: "double" occurring perhaps
six times in a total of several hundred entries; and once
very early in the list and followed by several marks of
exclamation, "total failure!!!" All this, though it whetted
my curiosity, told me little that was definite. Here were a
phial of some salt, and the record of a series of experiments that had led (like too many of Jekyll's investiga-

tions) to no end of practical usefulness. How could the presence of these articles in my home affect either the honour, the sanity, or the life of my flighty colleague? If his messenger could go to one place, why could he not go to another? And even granting some impediment, why was this gentleman to be received by me in secret? The more I reflected the more convinced I grew that I was dealing with a case of cerebral disease; and though I dismissed my servants to bed, I loaded an old revolver, that I might be found in some posture of self-defence.

Twelve o'clock had scarce rung out over London, ere the knocker sounded very gently on the door. I went myself at the summons, and found a small man crouching against the pillars of the portico.

"Are you come from Dr. Jekyll?" I asked.

He told me "yes" by a constrained gesture; and when I had bidden him enter, he did not obey me without a searching backward glance into the darkness of the square. There was a policeman not far off, advancing with his bull's eye open; and at the sight, I thought my visitor started and made greater haste.

These particulars struck me, I confess, disagreeably; and as I followed him into the bright light of the consulting room, I kept my hand ready on my weapon. Here, at last, I had a chance of clearly seeing him. I had never set eyes on him before, so much was certain. He was small, as I have said; I was struck besides with the shocking expression of his face, with his remarkable combination of great muscular activity and great apparent debility of constitution, and—last but not least—with the odd, subjective disturbance caused by his neighbourhood. This bore some resemblance to incipient rigour, and was accompanied by a marked sinking of the pulse. At the time, I set it down to some idiosyncratic, personal distaste, and merely wondered at the acuteness of the symptoms; but

I have since had reason to believe the cause to lie much deeper in the nature of man, and to turn on some nobler hinge than the principle of hatred.

This person (who had thus, from the first moment of his entrance, struck in me what I can only describe as a disgustful curiosity) was dressed in a fashion that would have made an ordinary person laughable; his clothes, that is to say, although they were of rich and sober fabric, were enormously too large for him in every measurement— the trousers hanging on his legs and rolled up to keep them from the ground, the waist of the coat below his haunches, and the collar sprawling wide upon his shoulders. Strange to relate, this ludicrous accoutrement was far from moving me to laughter. Rather, as there was something abnormal and misbegotten in the very essence of the creature that now faced me—something seizing, surprising and revolting—this fresh disparity seemed but to fit in with and to reinforce it; so that to my interest in the man's nature and character, there was added a curiosity as to his origin, his life, his fortune and status in the world.

These observations, though they have taken so great a space to be set down in, were yet the work of a few seconds. My visitor was, indeed, on fire with sombre excitement.

"Have you got it?" he cried. "Have you got it?" And so lively was his impatience that he even laid his hand upon my arm and sought to shake me.

I put him back, conscious at his touch of a certain icy pang along my blood. "Come, sir," said I. "You forget that I have not yet the pleasure of your acquaintance. Be seated, if you please." And I showed him an example, and sat down myself in my customary seat and with as fair an imitation of my ordinary manner to a patient, as the lateness of the hour, the nature of my preoccupations, and the horror I had of my visitor, would suffer me to muster.

"I beg your pardon, Dr. Lanyon," he replied civilly enough. "What you say is very well founded; and my impatience has shown its heels to my politeness. I come here at the instance of your colleague, Dr. Henry Jekyll, on a piece of business of some moment; and I understood . . ." He paused and put his hand to his throat, and I could see, in spite of his collected manner, that he was wrestling against the approaches of the hysteria—"I understand, a drawer . . ."

But here I took pity on my visitor's suspense, and some perhaps on my own growing curiosity.

"There it is, sir," said I, pointing to the drawer, where it lay on the floor behind a table and still covered with the sheet.

He sprang to it, and then paused, and laid his hand upon his heart: I could hear his teeth grate with the convulsive action of his jaws; and his face was so ghastly to see that I grew alarmed both for his life and reason.

"Compose yourself," said I.

He turned a dreadful smile to me, and as if with the decision of despair, plucked away the sheet. At sight of the contents, he uttered one loud sob of such immense relief that I sat petrified. And the next moment, in a voice that was already fairly well under control, "Have you a graduated glass?" he asked.

I rose from my place with something of an effort and gave him what he asked.

He thanked me with a smiling nod, measured out a few minims of the red tincture and added one of the powders. The mixture, which was at first a reddish hue, began, in proportion as the crystals melted, to brighten in colour, to effervesce audibly, and to throw off small fumes of vapour. Suddenly and at the same moment, the ebullition ceased and the compound changed to a dark purple, which faded again more slowly to a watery green. My visitor, who had watched these metamorphoses with a keen eye, smiled, set down the glass upon the table, and then turned and looked upon me with an air of scrutiny.

"And now," said he, "to settle what remains. Will you be wise? will you be guided? will you suffer me to take this glass in my hand and to go forth from your house without further parley? or has the greed of curiosity too much command of you? Think before you answer, for it shall be done as you decide. As you decide, you shall be left as you were before, and neither richer nor wiser, unless the sense of service rendered to a man in mortal distress may be counted as a kind of riches of the soul. Or, if you shall so prefer to choose, a new province of knowledge and new avenues to fame and power shall be laid open to you, in this room, upon the instant; and your sight shall be blasted by a prodigy to stagger the unbelief of Satan."

"Sir," said I, affecting a coolness that I was far from truly possessing, "you speak enigmas, and you will perhaps not wonder that I hear you with no very strong impression of belief. But I have gone too far in the way of inexplicable services to pause before I see the end."

"It is well," replied my visitor. "Lanyon, you remember your vows: what follows is under the seal of our profession. And now, you who have so long been bound to the most narrow and material views, you who have denied the virtue of transcendental medicine, you who have derided your superiors—behold!"

He put the glass to his lips and drank at one gulp. A cry followed; he reeled, staggered, clutched at the table and held on, staring with injected eyes, gasping with open mouth; and as I looked there came, I thought, a change—he seemed to swell—his face became suddenly black and the features seemed to melt and alter—and the next moment, I had sprung to my feet and leaped back against the wall, my arm raised to shield me from the prodigy, my mind submerged in terror.

"O God!" I screamed, and "O God!" again and again; for there before my eyes—pale and shaken, and half fainting, and groping before him with his hands, like a man restored from death—there stood Henry Jekyll!

What he told me in the next hour, I cannot bring my mind to set on paper. I saw what I saw, I heard what I heard, and my soul sickened at it; and yet now when that sight has faded from my eyes, I ask myself if I believe it, and I cannot answer. My life is shaken to its roots; sleep has left me; the deadliest terror sits by me at all hours of the day and night; and I feel that my days are numbered, and that I must die; and yet I shall die incredulous. As for the moral turpitude that man unveiled to me, even with tears of penitence, I cannot, even in memory, dwell on it without a start of horror. I will say but one thing, Utterson, and that (if you can bring your mind to credit it) will be more than enough. The creature who crept into my house that night was, on Jekyll's own confession, known by the name of Hyde and hunted for in every corner of the land as the murderer of Carew.

—Hastie Lanyon

Henry Jekyll's Full Statement
of the Case

I was born in the year 18— to a large fortune, endowed besides with excellent parts, inclined by nature to industry, fond of the respect of the wise and good among my fellowmen, and thus, as might have been supposed, with every guarantee of an honourable and distinguished future. And indeed the worst of my faults was a certain impatient gaiety of disposition, such as has made the happiness of many, but such as I found it hard to reconcile with my imperious desire to carry my head high, and wear a more than commonly grave countenance before the public. Hence it came about that I concealed my pleasures; and that when I reached years of reflection, and began to look round me and take stock of my progress and position in the world, I stood already committed to a profound duplicity of life. Many a man would have even blazoned such irregularities as I was guilty of; but from the high views that I had set before me, I regarded and hid them with an almost morbid sense of shame. It was thus rather the exacting nature of my aspirations than any particular degradation in my faults, that made me what I was, and, with even a deeper trench than in the majority of men, severed in me those provinces of good and ill which divide and compound man's dual nature. In this case, I was driven to reflect deeply and inveterately on that hard law of life, which lies at the root of religion and is one of the most plentiful springs of distress. Though so profound a double-dealer, I was in no sense a hypocrite; both sides of me were in dead earnest; I was no more myself when I laid aside restraint and plunged in shame, than when I laboured, in the eye of day, at the furtherance of knowledge or the relief of sorrow and suffering. And it chanced that the direction of my scientific studies, which led wholly towards the mystic and the transcendental, reacted and shed a strong light on this consciousness of the perennial war among my members. With every day, and from both sides of my intelligence, the moral and the intellectual, I thus drew steadily nearer to that truth, by whose partial discovery I have been doomed to such a dreadful shipwreck: that man is not truly one, but truly two. I say two, because the state of my own knowledge does not pass beyond that point. Others will follow, others will outstrip me on the same lines; and I hazard the guess that man will be ultimately known for a mere polity of multifarious, incongruous and independent denizens. I, for my part, from the nature of my life, advanced infallibly in one direction and in one direction only. It was on the moral side, and in my own person, that I learned to recognise the thorough and primitive duality of man; I saw that, of the two natures that contended in the field of my consciousness, even if I could rightly be said to be either, it was only because I was radically both; and from an early date, even before the course of my scientific discoveries had begun to suggest the most naked possibility of such a miracle, I had learned to dwell with pleasure, as a beloved daydream, on the thought of the separation of these elements. If each, I told myself, could be housed in separate identities, life would be relieved of all that was unbearable; the unjust might go his way, delivered from the aspirations and remorse of his more upright twin; and the just could walk steadfastly and securely on his upward path, doing the good things in which he found his pleasure, and no longer exposed to disgrace and penitence by the hands of this extraneous evil. It was the curse of mankind that these incongruous faggots were thus bound together—that in the agonised womb of consciousness, these polar twins should be continuously struggling. How, then, were they dissociated?

I was so far in my reflections when, as I have said, a side light began to shine upon the subject from the laboratory table. I began to perceive more deeply than it has ever yet been stated, the trembling immateriality, the mist-like transience, of this seemingly so solid body in which we walk attired. Certain agents I found to have the power to shake and pluck back that fleshly vestment, even as a wind might toss the curtains of a pavilion. For two good reasons, I will not enter deeply into this scientific branch of my confession. First, because I have been made to learn that the doom and burthen of our life is bound forever on man's shoulder, and when the attempt is made to cast it off, it but returns upon us with more unfamiliar and more awful pressure. Second, because, as my narrative will make, alas! too evident, my discoveries were incomplete. Enough then, that I not only recognised my natural body from the mere aura and effulgence of certain of the powers that made up my spirit, but managed to compound a drug by which these powers should be dethroned from their supremacy, and a second form and countenance substituted, none the less natural to me because they were the expression, and bore the stamp of lower elements in my soul.

I hesitated long before I put this theory to the test of

practise. I knew well that I risked death; for any drug that so potently controlled and shook the very fortress of identity might, by the least scruple of an overdose or at the least inopportunity in the moment of exhibition, utterly blot out that immaterial tabernacle which I looked to it to change. But the temptation of a discovery so singular and profound at last overcame the suggestions of alarm. I had long since prepared my tincture; I purchased at once, from a firm of wholesale chemists, a large quantity of a particular salt which I knew, from my experiments, to be the last ingredient required; and late one accursed night, I compounded the elements, watched them boil and smoke together in the glass, and when the ebullition had subsided, with a strong glow of courage, drank off the potion.

The most racking pangs succeeded: a grinding in the bones, deadly nausea, and a horror of the spirit that cannot be exceeded at the hour of birth or death. Then these agonies began swiftly to subside, and I came to myself as if out of a great sickness. There was something strange in my sensations, something indescribably new and, from its very novelty, incredibly sweet. I felt younger, lighter, happier in body; within I was conscious of a heady recklessness, a current of disordered sensual images running like a mill-race in my fancy, a solution of the bonds of obligation, an unknown but not an innocent freedom of the soul. I knew myself, at the first breath of this new life, to be more wicked, tenfold more wicked, sold a slave to my original evil; and the thought, in that moment, braced and delighted me like wine. I stretched out my hands, exulting in the freshness of these sensations; and in the act, I was suddenly aware that I had lost in stature.

There was no mirror, at that date, in my room; that which stands beside me as I write, was brought there later on and for the very purpose of these transformations. The night, however, was far gone into the morning—the morning, black as it was, was nearly ripe for the conception of the day—the inmates of my house were locked in the most rigorous hours of slumber; and I determined, flushed as I was with hope and triumph, to venture in my new shape as far as to my bedroom. I crossed the yard, wherein the constellations looked down upon me, I could have thought, with wonder, the first creature of that sort that their unsleeping vigilance had yet disclosed to them; I stole through the corridors, a stranger in my own house; and coming to my room, I saw for the first time the appearance of Edward Hyde.

I must here speak by theory alone, saying not that which I know, but which I suppose to be most probable. The evil side of my nature, to which I had now transferred the stamping efficacy, was less robust and less developed than the good which I had just deposed. Again, in the course of my life, which had been, after all, nine tenths a life of effort, virtue and control, it had been much less exercised and much less exhausted. And hence, as I think, it came about that Edward Hyde was so much smaller, slighter and younger than Henry Jekyll. Even as good shone upon the countenance of the one, evil was written broadly and plainly on the face of the other. Evil besides (which I must still believe to be the lethal side of man) had left on that body an imprint of deformity and decay. And yet when I looked upon that ugly idol in the glass, I was conscious of no repugnance, rather of a leap of welcome. This, too, was myself. It seemed natural and human. In my eyes it bore a livelier image of the spirit, it seemed more express and single, than the imperfect and divided countenance I had been hitherto accustomed to call mine. And in so far I was doubtless right. I have observed that when I wore the semblance of Edward Hyde, none could come near to me at first without a visible misgiving of the flesh. This, as I take it, was because all human beings, as we meet them, are commingled out of good and evil: and Edward Hyde, alone in the ranks of mankind, was pure evil.

I lingered but a moment at the mirror: the second and conclusive experiment had yet to be attempted; it yet remained to be seen if I had lost my identity beyond redemption and must flee before daylight from a house that was no longer mine; and hurrying back to my cabinets, I once more prepared and drank the cup, once more suffered the pangs of dissolution, and came to myself once more with the character, the stature and face of Henry Jekyll.

That night I had come to the fatal cross-roads. Had I approached my discovery in a more noble spirit, had I risked the experiment while under the empire of generous or pious aspirations, all must have been otherwise, and from these agonies of death and birth, I had come forth an angel instead of a fiend. The drug had no discriminating action; it was neither diabolical nor divine; it but shook the doors of the prisonhouse of my disposition; and like the captives of Philippi, that which stood within ran forth. At that time my virtue slumbered; my evil, kept awake by ambition, was alert and swift to seize the occasion; and the thing that was projected was Edward Hyde. Hence, although I had now two characters as well as two appearances, one was wholly evil, and the other was still the old Henry Jekyll, that incongruous compound of whose reformation and improvement I had already learned to despair. The movement was thus wholly toward the worse.

Even at that time, I had not conquered my aversions to the dryness of a life of study. I would still be merrily disposed at times; and as my pleasures were (to say the least) undignified, and I was not only well known and highly considered, but growing towards the elderly man, this incoherency of my life was daily growing more unwelcome. It was on this side that my new power tempted me until I fell in slavery. I had but to drink the cup, to doff at once the body of the noted professor, and to assume, like a thick cloak, that of Edward Hyde. I smiled at the notion; it seemed to me at the time to be humourous; and I made my preparations with the most studious care. I took and furnished that house in Soho, to which Hyde was tracked by the police; and engaged as a housekeeper a creature whom I knew well to be silent and unscrupulous. On the other side, I announced to my servants that a Mr. Hyde (whom I described) was to have full liberty and power about my house in the square; and to parry mishaps, I even called and made myself a familiar object, in my second character. I next drew up that will to which you so much objected; so that if anything befell me in the person of Dr. Jekyll, I could enter on that of Edward Hyde without pecuniary loss. And thus fortified, as I supposed, on every side, I began to profit by the strange immunities of my position.

Men have before hired bravos to transact their crimes, while their own person and reputation sat under shelter. I was the first that ever did so for his pleasures. I was the first that could plod in the public eye with a load of genial respectability, and in a moment, like a schoolboy, strip off these lendings and spring headlong into the sea of liberty. But for me, in my impenetrable mantle, the safety was complete. Think of it—I did not even exist! Let me but escape into my laboratory door, give me but a second or two to mix and swallow the draught that I had always standing ready; and whatever he had done, Edward Hyde would pass away like the stain of breath upon a mirror; and there in his stead, quietly at home, trimming the midnight lamp in his study, a man who could afford to laugh at suspicion, would be Henry Je-kyll.

The pleasures which I made haste to seek in my dis-guise were, as I have said, undignified; I would scarce use a harder term. But in the hands of Edward Hyde, they soon began to turn toward the monstrous. When I would come back from these excursions, I was often plunged into a kind of wonder at my vicarious depravity. This fa-miliar that I called out of my own soul, and sent forth alone to do his good pleasure, was a being inherently malign and villainous; his every act and thought centered on self; drinking pleasure with bestial avidity from any degree of torture to another; relentless like a man of stone. Henry Jekyll stood at times aghast before the acts of Edward Hyde; but the situation was apart from ordi-nary laws, and insidiously relaxed the grasp of con-science. It was Hyde, after all, and Hyde alone, that was guilty. Jekyll was no worse; he woke again to his good qualities seemingly unimpaired; he would even make haste, where it was possible, to undo the evil done by Hyde. And thus his conscience slumbered.

Into the details of the infamy at which I thus connived (for even now I can scarce grant that I committed it) I have no design of entering; I mean but to point out the warnings and the successive steps with which my chas-tisement approached. I met with one accident which, as it brought on no consequence, I shall no more than men-tion. An act of cruelty to a child aroused against me the anger of a passer-by, whom I recognised the other day in the person of your kinsman; the doctor and the child's family joined him; there were moments when I feared for my life; and at last, in order to pacify their too just resentment, Edward Hyde had to bring them to the door, and pay them in a cheque drawn in the name of Henry Jekyll. But this danger was easily eliminated from the future, by opening an account at another bank in the name of Edward Hyde himself; and when, by sloping my own hand backward, I had supplied my double with a signature, I thought I sat beyond the reach of fate.

Some two months before the murder of Sir Danvers, I had been out for one of my adventures, had returned at a late hour, and woke the next day in bed with somewhat odd sensations. It was in vain I looked about me; in vain I saw the decent furniture and tall proportions of my room in the square; in vain that I recognised the pattern of the bed curtains and the design of the mahogany frame; something still kept insisting that I was not where I was, that I had not wakened where I seemed to be, but in the little room in Soho where I was accustomed to sleep in the body of Edward Hyde. I smiled to myself, and, in my psychological way, began lazily to inquire into the elements of this illusion, occasionally, even as I did so, dropping back into a comfortable morning doze. I was still so engaged when, in one of my more wakeful moments, my eyes fell upon my hand. Now the hand of Henry Jekyll (as you have often remarked) was professional in shape and size: it was large, firm, white and comely. But the hand which I now saw, clearly enough, in the yellow light of a mid-London morning, lying half shut on the bedclothes, was lean, corded, knuckly, of a dusky pallor and thickly shaded with a swart growth of hair. It was the hand of Edward Hyde.

I must have stared upon it for near half a minute, sunk as I was in the mere stupidity of wonder, before terror woke up in my breast as sudden and startling as the crash of cymbals; and bounding from my bed, I rushed to the mirror. At the sight that met my eyes, my blood was changed into something exquisitely thin and icy. Yes, I had gone to bed Henry Jekyll, I had awakened Edward Hyde. How was this to be explained? I asked myself; and then, with another bound of terror—how was it to be remedied? It was well on in the morning; the servants were up; all my drugs were in the cabinet—a long journey down two pairs of stairs, through the back passage, across the open court and through the anatomical theatre, from where I was then standing horror-struck. It might indeed be possible to cover my face; but of what use was that, when I was unable to conceal the alteration of my stature? And then with an overpowering sweetness of relief, it came back upon my mind that the servants were already used to the coming and going of my second self. I had soon dressed, as well as I was able, in clothes of my own size: had soon passed through the house, where Bradshaw stared and drew back at seeing Mr. Hyde at such an hour and in such a strange array; and ten minutes later, Dr. Jekyll had returned to his own shape and was sitting down, with a darkened brow, to make a feint of breakfasting.

Small indeed was my appetite. This inexplicable incident, this reversal of my previous experience, seemed, like the Babylonian finger on the wall, to be spelling out the letters of my judgment; and I began to reflect more seriously than ever before on the issues and possibilities of my double existence. That part of me which I had the power of projecting, had lately been much exercised and nourished; it had seemed to me of late as though the body of Edward Hyde had grown in stature, as though (when I wore that form) I were conscious of a more generous tide of blood; and I began to spy a danger that, if this were much prolonged, the balance of my nature might be permanently overthrown, the power of voluntary change be forfeited, and the character of Edward Hyde become irrevocably mine. The power of the drug had not been always equally displayed. Once, very early in my careers, it had totally failed me; since then I had been obliged on more than one occasion to double, and once, with infinite risk of death, to treble the amount; and these rare uncertainties had cast hitherto the sole shadow on my contentment. Now, however, and in the light of that morning's accident, I was led to remark that whereas, in the beginning, the difficulty had been to throw off the body of Jekyll, it had of late gradually but decidedly transferred itself to the other side. All things therefore seemed to point to this; that I was slowly losing hold of my original and better self, and becoming slowly incorporated with my second and worse.

Between these two, I now felt I had to choose. My two natures had memory in common, but all other faculties were most unequally shared between them. Jekyll (who was composite) now with the most sensitive apprehensions, now with a greedy gusto, projected and shared in the pleasures and adventures of Hyde; but Hyde was indifferent to Jekyll, or but remembered him as the mountain bandit remembers the cavern in which he conceals himself from pursuit. Jekyll had more than a father's interest; Hyde had more of a son's indifference. To cast in my lot with Jekyll, was to die to those appetites which I had long secretly indulged and had of late begun to pamper. To cast it in with Hyde, was to die to a thousand interests and aspirations, and to become, at a blow and forever, despised and friendless. The bargain might appear unequal; but there was still another consideration in the scales; for while Jekyll would suffer smartingly in the fires of abstinence, Hyde would be not even conscious of all that he had lost. Strange as my circumstances were, the terms of this debate are as old and commonplace as man; much the same inducements and alarms cast the die for any tempted and trembling sinner; and it fell out with me, as it falls with so vast a majority of my fellows, that I chose the better part and was found wanting in the strength to keep to it.

Yes, I preferred the elderly and discontented doctor, surrounded by friends and cherishing honest hopes; and bade a resolute farewell to the liberty, the comparative youth, the light step, leaping impulses and secret pleasures, that I had enjoyed in the disguise of Hyde. I made this choice perhaps with some unconscious reservation, for I neither gave up the house in Soho, nor destroyed the clothes of Edward Hyde, which still lay ready in my cabinet. For two months, however, I was true to my determination; for two months, I led a life of such severity as I had never before attained to, and enjoyed the compensations of an approving conscience. But time began at last to obliterate the freshness of my alarm; the praises of conscience began to grow into a thing of course; I began to be tortured with throes and longings, as of Hyde struggling for freedom; and at last, in an hour of moral weakness, I once again compounded and swallowed the transforming draught.

I do not suppose that, when a drunkard reasons with himself upon his vice, he is once out of five hundred times affected by the dangers that he runs through his brutish, physical insensibility; neither had I, long as I had considered my position, made enough allowance for the complete moral insensibility and insensate readiness to evil, which were the leading characters of Edward Hyde. Yet it was by these that I was punished. My devil had been long caged, he came out roaring. I was conscious, even when I took the draught, of a more unbridled, a more furious propensity to ill. It must have been this, I suppose, that stirred in my soul that tempest of impatience with which I listened to the civilities of my unhappy victim; I declare, at least, before God, no man morally sane could have been guilty of that crime upon so pitiful a provocation; and that I struck in no more reasonable spirit than that in which a sick child may break a plaything. But I had voluntarily stripped myself of all those balancing instincts by which even the worst of us continues to walk with some degree of steadiness among temptations; and in my case, to be tempted, however slightly, was to fall.

Instantly the spirit of hell awoke in me and raged. With a transport of glee, I mauled the unresisting body, tasting delight from every blow; and it was not till weariness had begun to succeed, that I was suddenly, in the top fit of my delirium, struck through the heart by a cold thrill of terror. A mist dispersed; I saw my life to be forfeit; and fled from the scene of these excesses, at once glorying and trembling, my lust of evil gratified and stimulated, my love of life screwed to the topmost peg. I ran to the house in Soho, and (to make assurance doubly sure) destroyed my papers; thence I set out through the lamplit streets, in the same divided ecstasy of mind, gloating on my crime, light-headedly devising others in the future, and yet still hastening and still hearkening in my wake for the steps of the avenger. Hyde had a song upon his lips as he compounded the draught, and as he drank it, pledged the dead man. The pangs of transformation had not done tearing him, before Henry Jekyll, with streaming tears of gratitude and remorse, had fallen upon his knees and lifted his clasped hands to God. The veil of self-indulgence was rent from head to foot. I saw my life as a whole: I followed it up from the days of childhood, when I had walked with my father's hand, and through the self-denying toils of my professional life, to arrive again and again, with the same sense of unreality, at the damned horrors of the evening. I could have screamed aloud; I sought with tears and prayers to

smother down the crowd of hideous images and sounds
with which my memory swarmed against me; and still,
between the petitions, the ugly face of my iniquity stared
into my soul. As the acuteness of this remorse began to
die away, it was succeeded by a sense of joy. The problem
of my conduct was solved. Hyde was thenceforth impossible; whether I would or not, I was now confined to the
better part of my existence; and O, how I rejoiced to
think of it! with what willing humility I embraced anew
the restrictions of natural life! with what sincere renun-
ciation I locked the door by which I had so often gone
and come, and ground the key under my heel!

The next day, came the news that the murder had
been overlooked, that the guilt of Hyde was patent to
the world, and that the victim was a man high in public
estimation. It was not only a crime, it had been a tragic
folly. I think I was glad to know it; I think I was glad to
have my better impulses thus buttressed and guarded by
the terrors of the scaffold. Jekyll was now my city of refuge; let but Hyde peep out an instant, and the hands of
all men would be raised to take and slay him.

I resolved in my future conduct to redeem the past;
and I can say with honesty that my resolve was fruitful
of some good. You know yourself how earnestly, in the
last months of the last year, I laboured to relieve suffering; you know that much was done for others, and that
the days passed quietly, almost happily for myself. Nor
can I truly say that I wearied of this beneficent and innocent life; I think instead that I daily enjoyed it more
completely; but I was still cursed with my duality of purpose; and as the first edge of my penitence wore off, the
lower side of me, so long indulged, so recently chained
down, began to growl for licence. Not that I dreamed of
resuscitating Hyde; the bare idea of that would startle
me to frenzy: no, it was in my own person that I was once

more tempted to trifle with my conscience; and it was as an ordinary secret sinner that I at last fell before the assaults of temptation.

There comes an end to all things; the most capacious measure is filled at last; and this brief condescension to my evil finally destroyed the balance of my soul. And yet I was not alarmed; the fall seemed natural, like a return to the old days before I had made my discovery. It was a fine, clear, January day, wet under foot where the frost had melted, but cloudless overhead; and the Regent's Park was full of winter chirrupings and sweet with spring odours. I sat in the sun on a bench; the animal within me licking the chops of memory; the spiritual side a little drowsed, promising subsequent penitence, but not yet moved to begin. After all, I reflected, I was like my neighbours; and then I smiled, comparing myself with the other men, comparing my active good-will with the lazy cruelty of their neglect. And at the very moment of that vainglorious thought, a qualm came over me, a horrid nausea and the most deadly shuddering. These passed away, and left me faint; and then as in its turn faintness subsided, I began to be aware of a change in the temper of my thoughts, a greater boldness, a contempt of danger, a solution of the bonds of obligation. I looked down; my clothes hung formlessly on my shrunken limbs; the hand that lay on my knee was corded and hairy. I was once more Edward Hyde. A moment before I had been safe of all men's respect, wealthy, beloved—the cloth laying for me in the dining-room at home; and now I was the common quarry of mankind, hunted, houseless, a known murderer, thrall to the gallows.

My reason wavered, but it did not fail me utterly. I have more than once observed that, in my second character, my faculties seemed sharpened to a point and my spirits more tensely elastic; thus it came about that, where Jekyll perhaps might have succumbed, Hyde rose to the importance of the moment. My drugs were in one of the presses of my cabinet; how was I to reach them? That was the problem that (crushing my temples in my hands) I set myself to solve. The laboratory door I had closed. If I sought to enter by the house, my own servants would consign me to the gallows. I saw I must employ another hand, and thought of Lanyon. How was he to be reached? how persuaded? Supposing that I escaped capture in the streets, how was I to make my way into his presence? and how should I, an unknown and displeasing visitor, prevail on the famous physician to rifle the study of his colleague, Dr. Jekyll? Then I remembered that of my original character, one part remained to me: I could write my own hand; and once I had conceived that kindling spark, the way that I must follow became lighted up from end to end.

Thereupon, I arranged my clothes as best I could, and summoning a passing hansom, drove to an hotel in Portland Street, the name of which I chanced to remember. At my appearance (which was indeed comical enough, however tragic a fate these garments covered) the driver could not conceal his mirth. I gnashed my teeth upon him with a gust of devilish fury; and the smile withered from his face—happily for him—yet more happily for myself, for in another instant I had certainly dragged him from his perch. At the inn, as I entered, I looked about me with so black a countenance as made the attendants tremble; not a look did they exchange in my presence; but obsequiously took my orders, led me to a private room, and brought me wherewithal to write. Hyde in danger of his life was a creature new to me; shaken with inordinate anger, strung to the pitch of murder, lusting to inflict pain. Yet the creature was astute; mastered his fury with a great effort of the will; composed two important letters, one to Lanyon and one to Poole; and that he might receive actual evidence of their being posted, sent them out with directions that they should be registered. Thenceforward, he sat all day over the fire in the private room, gnawing his nails; there he dined, sitting alone with his fears, the waiter visibly quailing before his eye; and thence, when the night was fully come, he set forth in the corner of a closed cab, and was driven to and fro about the streets of the city. He, I say—I cannot say, I. That child of Hell had nothing human; nothing lived in him but fear and hatred. And when at last, thinking the driver had begun to grow suspicious, he discharged the cab and ventured on foot, attired in his misfitting clothes, an object marked out for observation, into the midst of the nocturnal passengers, these two base passions raged within him like a tempest. He walked fast, hunted by his fears, chattering to himself, skulking through the less frequented thoroughfares, counting the minutes that still divided him from midnight. Once a woman spoke to him, offering, I think, a box of lights. He smote her in the face, and she fled.

When I came to myself at Lanyon's, the horror of my old friend perhaps affected me somewhat: I do not know; it was at least but a drop in the sea to the abhorrence with which I looked back upon these hours. A change had come over me. It was no longer the fear of the gallows, it was the horror of being Hyde that racked me. I received Lanyon's condemnation partly in a dream; it was partly in a dream that I came home to my own house and got into bed. I slept after the prostration of the day, with a stringent and profound slumber which not even the nightmares that wrung me could avail to break. I awoke in the morning shaken, weakened, but refreshed. I still hated and feared the thought of the brute that slept within me, and I had not of course forgotten the appalling dangers of the day before; but I was once more at home, in my own house and close to my drugs; and gratitude for my escape shone so strong in my soul that it almost rivalled the brightness of hope.

I was stepping leisurely across the court after breakfast, drinking the chill of the air with pleasure, when I was seized again with those indescribable sensations that heralded the change; and I had but the time to gain the shelter of my cabinet, before I was once again raging and freezing with the passions of Hyde. It took on this occasion a double dose to recall me to myself; and alas! six hours after, as I sat looking sadly in the fire, the pangs returned, and the drug had to be re-administered. In short, from that day forth it seemed only by a great effort as of gymnastics, and only under the immediate stimulation of the drug, that I was able to wear the countenance of Jekyll. At all hours of the day and night, I would be taken with the premonitory shudder; above all, if I slept, or even dozed for a moment in my chair, it was always as Hyde that I awakened. Under the strain of this continually impending doom and by the sleeplessness to which I now condemned myself, ay, even beyond what I had thought possible to man, I became, in my own person, a creature eaten up and emptied by fever, languidly weak both in body and mind, and solely occupied by one thought: the horror of my other self. But when I slept, or when the virtue of the medicine wore off, I would leap almost without transition (for the pangs of transformation grew daily less marked) into the possession of a fancy brimming with images of terror, a soul boiling with causeless hatreds, and a body that seemed not strong enough to contain the raging energies of life. The powers of Hyde seemed to have grown with the sickliness of Jekyll. And certainly the hate that now divided them was equal on each side. With Jekyll, it was a thing of vital

instinct. He had now seen the full deformity of that creature that shared with him some of the phenomena of
consciousness, and was co-heir with him to death: and
beyond these links of community, which in themselves
made the most poignant part of his distress, he thought
of Hyde, for all his energy of life, as of something not
only hellish but inorganic. This was the shocking thing;
that the slime of the pit seemed to utter cries and voices;
that the amorphous dust gesticulated and sinned; that
what was dead, and had no shape, should usurp the offices of life. And this again, that that insurgent horror
was knit to him closer than a wife, closer than an eye; lay
caged in his flesh, where he heard it mutter and felt it
struggle to be born; and at every hour of weakness, and
in the confidence of slumber, prevailed against him, and
deposed him out of life. The hatred of Hyde for Jekyll
was of different order. His terror of the gallows drove
him continually to commit temporary suicide, and return
to his subordinate station of a part instead of a person;
but he loathed the necessity, he loathed the despondency
into which Jekyll was now fallen, and he resented the
dislike with which he was himself regarded. Hence the
ape-like tricks that he would play me, scrawling in my
own hand blasphemies on the pages of my books, burn-
ing the letters and destroying the portrait of my father;
and indeed, had it not been for his fear of death, he
would long ago have ruined himself in order to involve
me in the ruin. But his love of life is wonderful; I go further: I, who sicken and freeze at the mere thought of him,
when I recall the abjection and passion of this attach-
ment, and when I know how he fears my power to cut
him off by suicide, I find it in my heart to pity him.

It is useless, and the time awfully fails me, to prolong
this description; no one has ever suffered such torments,
let that suffice; and yet even to these, habit brought—no,

not alleviation—but a certain callousness of soul, a certain acquiescence of despair; and my punishment might have gone on for years, but for the last calamity which has now fallen, and which has finally severed me from my own face and nature. My provision of the salt, which had never been renewed since the date of the first experiment, began to run low. I sent out for a fresh supply and mixed the draught; the ebullition followed, and the first change of colour, not the second; I drank it and it was without efficiency. You will learn from Poole how I have had London ransacked; it was in vain; and I am now persuaded that my first supply was impure, and that it was that unknown impurity which lent efficacy to the draught.

About a week has passed, and I am now finishing this statement under the influence of the last of the old powders. This, then, is the last time, short of a miracle, that Henry Jekyll can think his own thoughts or see his own face (now how sadly altered!) in the glass. Nor must I delay too long to bring my writing to an end; for if my narrative has hitherto escaped destruction, it has been by a combination of great prudence and great good luck. Should the throes of change take me in the act of writing it, Hyde will tear it in pieces; but if some time shall have elapsed after I have laid it by, his wonderful selfishness and circumscription to the moment will probably save it once again from the action of his ape-like spite. And indeed the doom that is closing on us both has already changed and crushed him. Half an hour from now, when I shall again and forever reindue that hated personality, I know how I shall sit shuddering and weeping in my chair, or continue, with the most strained and fearstruck ecstasy of listening, to pace up and down this room (my last earthly refuge) and give ear to every sound of menace. Will Hyde die upon the scaffold? or will he find courage to release himself at the last moment? God knows; I am careless; this is my true hour of death, and what is to follow concerns another than myself. Here then, as I lay down the pen and proceed to seal up my confession, I bring the life of that unhappy Henry Jekyll to an end.

AFTERWORD

Vladimir Nabokov starts his introduction to *Dr. Jekyll and Mr. Hyde* with an injunction, telling us that we should "completely forget, disremember, unlearn, consign to oblivion" any of our assumptions about this book. But it's hard to do, isn't it? Like Frankenstein's monster, like Dracula, like the Werewolf and the Mummy, Jekyll/Hyde is an icon of horror, a Halloween staple. Perhaps as children we even played pretend, acting out the drama of the mad scientist: holding the test tube bubbling with a noxious green liquid, which we drink; putting a hand to our throats as our mouths constrict, grimacing. We imagined the moment of transformation—perhaps thick hair sprouted; perhaps the skin turned a sickly color; perhaps the brow extended, apelike, and the lips sneered over crooked teeth. Probably we thrashed around, and something in the laboratory fell crashing to the floor, no doubt shattering dramatically. And then came the evil maniacal laughter.

If you were alive in the century that followed the publication of this novel, it's likely that you encountered the basics of Stevenson's story dozens upon dozens of times, even if you never touched the book itself. For more than a hundred years, it's been a part of the cultural air around us. There have been at least ninety films based upon the text, as well as many stage shows, comic books, jokes, media references, etc., so that the *idea* of Dr. Jekyll and Mr. Hyde is as much a piece of the collective unconscious as it is a book.

We probably first encountered a parody of the story as children—via Sylvester the Cat and Tweety Bird in the cartoon short "Dr. Jekyll's Hyde" or via an episode of the animated series *Pinky and the Brain.* Maybe we saw a comic film with Abbott and Costello (*Abbott and Costello Meet Dr. Jekyll and Mr. Hyde*) or Jerry Lewis (*The Nutty Professor*) or Eddie Murphy (*The Nutty Professor* remake). Maybe we saw the episode of TV's *Gilligan's Island* in which Gilligan dreams he has transformed into the murderous Hyde and bumps off the other castaways one by one.

As we grew up, we were no doubt at least vaguely aware of the imagery from Rouben Mamoulian's 1932 film version, even if we hadn't actually seen the movie. Fredric March won an Academy Award for his performance as Jekyll/Hyde, and it's *his* Hyde, rather than Stevenson's, who still exists most firmly in the public imagination—that face somewhere between that of an ugly street thug and that of a caveman, with a nasty crooked overbite and a disturbing shock of unkempt hair and gleefully malevolent eyes.

Still, decade after decade, subsequent generations of actors gamely took on the challenge of the role of the doomed Dr. Jekyll—from Spencer Tracy (1941) to Jack Palance (1968) and John Malkovich (1996). The part has been given twists over the years, and each era has often brought a new, "socially relevant" slant to the old story. We may have seen the solemnly Freudian Victor Fleming 1941 version, or the 1976 blaxploitation flick called

Dr. Black, Mr. Hyde, in which the African-American protagonist (Bernie Casey) is turned into a Caucasian who can't control his murderous impulses; or the 1995 *Dr. Jekyll and Ms. Hyde,* in which the doctor gets to find out what it feels like to be a beautiful woman and explore his sexuality. We may have attended a performance of the 1997 Broadway musical *Jekyll and Hyde* and emerged from the theater humming such tunes as "This Is the Moment" and "Murder, Murder."

Disremember, Nabokov says. *Consign to oblivion.*
Is he serious?

Maybe he is. Actually, a contemporary reader coming for the first time to Robert Louis Stevenson's *Dr. Jekyll and Mr. Hyde* may, in fact, be surprised. It's not quite what one expects. It is a fragmented, quietly feverish little book—a *sneaky* book. It proceeds through indirection, doling out sly hints but leaving, for the most part, the sordid facts to the imagination.

We begin in a place that is unfamiliar to those who know the story only through rumor and cultural static. There is the introduction of the lawyer Utterson, "a man of a rugged countenance that was never lighted by a smile; cold, scanty and embarrassed in discourse; backward in sentiment; lean, long, dusty, dreary and yet somehow lovable." The word "somehow" is of course a problematic one for a writer—a word that often signifies nothing so much as the writer's lazy inability to be specific. Yet it is a word that will appear frequently throughout *Dr. Jekyll.* Utterson, we are told, is *somehow* lovable, and in this first sentence, the foggy, tentative, strangely lacunar tone of the book is established.

We continue on down the page, perhaps a little puzzled, walking along with these two stodgy, reserved men, Utterson and Enfield—"It was reported by those who encountered them in their Sunday walks, that they said nothing, looked singularly dull. . . ." They walk past a dingy neighborhood, "a by-street in a busy quarter of London," and pass by a certain door that Enfield recognizes, "connected in my mind," Enfield says, "with a very odd story."

Okay. Now we're getting somewhere. Out of their stiff conversation emerges a piece of *Dr. Jekyll and Mr. Hyde* that we probably remember vividly from the movies: The image of Mr. Hyde deliberately running down a young girl in the street, trampling over her. We may recall having seen this moment dramatized. We may believe that it happens in a vivid, specific scene.

But it doesn't. It comes obliquely, in conversation, and the scene isn't so much described as referred to. *Somehow. Something.* There are other oddities to the narration, as well. Enfield says he "was coming home from some place at the end of the world, about three o'clock of a black winter morning" when he saw the scene with Hyde and the little girl. An attentive reader pauses for a moment. What does that mean—*some place at the end of the world*? And what is a little girl doing "running as hard as she was able down a cross street" at three in the morning? Even in these first few pages, there is a shadiness, a subtle uncertainty that begins to cast doubt on the solidity of the narrative. We can sense a more honest version of the tale sliding along, unspoken, beneath the surface.

We never do find out what Enfield was doing walking through this part of town in the dead of night, a part of town where "a man listens and listens and begins to long for the sight of a policeman," and we never get a real, solid description of Hyde from Enfield, either: "There is something wrong with his appearance," he says, "something displeasing, something down-right detestable. I never saw a man I so disliked, and yet I scarce know why. He must be deformed somewhere. . . ."

Even at this early point, the reader may begin to notice a pattern of evasiveness emerging, the *something*s and *somehow*s leaving blurred spots in our vision, like the fog that hangs over the London of this story, the fog that, as Utterson observes, "even in the houses . . . began to lie thickly." The book is full of polite silences, fey suggestions. We never find out what might cause Utterson to brood "on his own past, groping in all corners of memory, lest by chance some Jack-in-the-Box of an old iniquity should leap to light there." Beyond the incident that Enfield describes, and the subsequent murder of Sir Danvers Carew—observed by a maidservant from a distant window and reported in the novel secondhand—we never do find out, exactly, what Jekyll *does* in the guise of Hyde. All those hours he spends "drinking pleasure with bestial avidity from any degree of torture to another; relentless like a man of stone" are left to the reader's own uneasy dreams.

The structure of *The Strange Case of Dr. Jekyll and Mr. Hyde* follows a path as indirect and elusive as its multiple narrative voices. With its obliquely recorded incidents, its eyewitness accounts and sealed confessions, it resembles nothing so much as a casebook—a collection of gathered clues, fragments, through which the clever detective may be able to intuit or project a complete narrative. Perhaps one of the most compelling aspects of this novel is that, in fact, there's so much left here for us to fill in, so many scenes that we can only imagine.

Such a structure creates fertile ground for allegory hunters, and there are indeed many convincing interpretations of the novel. It's easy to picture it as a Christian parable about original evil that exists within us all, or as an illustration of the Freudian concepts of Ego and Id, the manifestation of Victorian sexual repression and hypocrisy. We can call the story a fable of addiction, with a junkie Jekyll in the end "crying night and day for some sort of medicine," sending out to pharmacies for "pure" samples of his drug. We can see Hyde as representing an anxiety of the underclass, with his Soho flat and his "lean, corded, knuckly" hand. We can see it as a reflection of Victorian ideas about evolution, with Mr. Hyde as a throwback to the primitive, precivilized ape cousin that Darwin's theories had evoked in the late-nineteenth-century imagination ("The man seems hardly human," Utterson thinks upon his first meeting with Hyde. "Something troglodytic, shall we say?") The puzzlelike structure of the novel creates for readers a kind of Rorschach test, open to a variety of interpretations.

Yet allegory is only compelling if it helps to explain some hidden aspect of our daily lives. *Dr. Jekyll and Mr. Hyde* was lucky to dovetail so nicely with both the radical ideas of the nineteenth century, such as Darwin's theories, but also with Freud, and with the twentieth century's fascination with the landscape of the mind. "I hazard the guess," Dr. Jekyll writes in his confession, "that man will ultimately be known for a mere polity of multifarious, incongruous and independent denizens."

It also happened that Stevenson's novel coincided rather closely with a series of murders that continue, even to this day, to capture the public imagination.

The famous Jack the Ripper killings occurred in the Whitechapel area of London in the late summer and early autumn of 1888, two years after the publication of *The Strange Case of Dr. Jekyll and Mr. Hyde*. Depending on which authority you consult, the Ripper murdered between four and nine women. No one was ever charged with the crimes.

By 1888, Stevenson's story was well-known. There were at least two stage versions of *The Strange Case of Dr. Jekyll and Mr. Hyde* being performed in London that year, including a musical farce based upon the story, which opened on September third, at the Royalty Theatre, three days after the first murder.

It seems likely that the Ripper, whoever he might have been, would have been familiar with Stevenson's story. Perhaps he even identified. This is idle speculation, it's true. Still, it's hard not to feel a little uncomfortable as we read Jekyll's ecstatic descriptions of becoming Hyde; he is suddenly "conscious of a heady recklessness, a current of disordered sensual images running like a millrace in my fancy, a solution of the bonds of obligation, an unknown but not an innocent freedom of the soul." Accurate or not, this passage has become a touchstone in the popular conception of the mind of a serial killer.

Jack the Ripper was not the first serial killer, of course, but he was perhaps the first to be presented as one, the first to appear when the general population was literate enough to follow the story of his deeds through the papers, the first to appear in the now familiar context of sensational journalism. The Ripper seemed aware of his murders as a kind of performance, leaving his victims in plain sight, sending taunting letters to the press, apparently enjoying the worldwide stir his crimes were causing. The public followed the search for the killer the way they would have followed a serialized novel, waiting impatiently for the next installment.

Given their proximity in time and tone, it's probably not surprising that over the course of the twentieth cen-

tury, popular representations of the Ripper have tended
to resemble images of Dr. Jekyll/Mr. Hyde. The two stories have often gone arm in arm in the public imagination, and frequently even the details of the two have
been recombined, mixed up. Many of the film versions of
Jekyll/Hyde have included a prostitute character or two,
for example—imported, apparently, from the Ripper
legend. Conversely, most of the film versions of the Ripper story present the killer as a Jekyll-like gentleman,
outwardly respectable—a split personality.

And then there is the iconic imagery itself. In both
cases, we are frequently presented with a picture of a
man in top hat and cape, a silhouette standing under a
gaslit streetlight. We might see a certain type of urban
street. A Cockney prostitute stands on a corner, a drunkard stumbles muttering into the gutter, and a horse-
drawn carriage *clip-clops* along the street. The alleyways
are dark. In both cases we imagine a gentleman transforming into a monster, lifting a walking stick or a surgeon's knife, slashing downward, brutally. Grinning.

Does the novel anticipate a murderer like Jack the Ripper? Does it have some prescient insight into psychopa-
thology? Well . . . not exactly. For the most part, the
novel is very much grounded in a Victorian sensibility.
The prose can be stodgy and florid, the attitudes both
prim and melodramatic. Yet at the same time, there are
intimations here of particularly modern concerns, and it
might be claimed that this book is among the first popular works to begin to articulate the sense of urban alien-
ation that would later become one of the primary
subjects of twentieth-century fiction.

Mr. Hyde could not exist without the modern city. He
needs the anonymity of the masses, and he needs the
newly gaslit streets, the flickering nighttime landscape of

pubs and brothels and beggars, the urban underworld that would later transform into the world of film noir. He needs an expanse of amoral territory to slink through, just as Jekyll needs a society in which his disaffection can go unnoticed, a world in which most neighbors are strangers.

"Men have before hired bravos to transact their crimes," Jekyll says in his confession. "I was the first that ever did so for his pleasures. I was the first that could plod in the public eye with a load of genial respectability, and in a moment, like a schoolboy, strip off these lendings, and spring headlong into the sea of liberty. But for me, in my impenetrable mantle, the safety was complete. Think of it—I did not even exist!"

The pleasures and terrors of this "sea of liberty" are perhaps more apparent to contemporary people than they were to the Victorians who first encountered this passage in Stevenson's book. We know that yearning quite well, don't we? We know that desire to dissolve into another identity entirely, to be reborn, to be incognito, and for us—with our new ease of mobility, with the constraints of class and rank loosened, in an age of anonymity—for us, it's more possible than ever to "spring headlong into that sea of liberty." This could well be the mantra of our nomadic age, the privilege of the overpopulated and estranged. *I did not even exist!* Jekyll exults, and in this single phrase he summarizes the great social change that was to overtake the civilized world in the upcoming century.

For modern readers, the Jekyll/Hyde legend seems to speak particularly to our nervousness about the solidity of the self. Who is the "real" me? What is the persona that people know as "me"? We are more self-conscious about the ordinary public masks that we naturally put on to negotiate our way through social interactions and the ways in which those masks separate us from the people in our lives we are supposed to be close to. One of the commonplaces of contemporary life is that sense that it's very easy to have a secret life. We know the old story: someone comes in and kills his coworkers with a semi-automatic. A serial killer spends years murdering folks and burying them in the crawl space beneath his house, and then later his acquaintances and coworkers are quite surprised. He's described as "quiet," "a nice guy." No one suspected. It's a familiar story that leads us all the way back to Jekyll's double life.

I did not even exist!

I thought of all of this again recently at the local amusement park. My nine-year-old son and I were standing in line among hundreds of thrill seekers, waiting for our chance at a ride called Mr. Hyde's Nasty Fall, and we casually discussed the novel—though my son had neither read it nor seen any of the movies. Still, he recognized that hirsute ogre in the top hat and Victorian cape; he knew that the counterpart was called Dr. Jekyll. He remembered the basics of the story, though he didn't know where, exactly, he had learned them.

"Why would you drink that potion, if you knew that it was going to turn you into a monster?" I asked, and my son looked at me sidelong.

"But it would be fun, too," he said. "I mean, you could get away with anything."

"That's true," I said. My son is not afraid of these rides, as I am, and he leaned back in the carriage as we were strapped in by the costumed attendant, before we began to ascend to the top. The faux-Cockney voice of Mr. Hyde spoke to us through a loudspeaker. "Step right up," he said, as we slowly rose, ten feet, fifty feet, one hundred twenty-five feet into the air. "I have something very interesting I want to show you," the Mr. Hyde voice said. We came to a stop at the pinnacle of the ride. "What would it be like if the cable on this elevator were to suddenly break?" Mr. Hyde whispered. "We're thirteen stories in the air now." My son smiled at my nervousness. He was pleasantly curious to know what it would feel like to be pushed down an elevator shaft by a giggling sociopath, and we braced ourselves.

"Have a nice fall," the loudspeaker Mr. Hyde cackled, and my son and I plunged together, screaming.

—Dan Chaon

Selected Bibliography

Prose Works by Robert Louis Stevenson

An Inland Voyage, 1878 Travel Book
Edinburgh: Picturesque Notes, 1879 Travel Book
Travels with a Donkey in the Cévennes, 1879 Travel Book
Virginibus Puerisque, 1881 Essays
Familiar Studies of Men and Books, 1882 Essays
New Arabian Nights, 1882 Stories
The Silverado Squatters, 1883 Travel Book
Treasure Island, 1883 Novel
More New Arabian Nights, The Dynamiter (with Fanny Van
    de Grift Stevenson), 1885 Stories
Prince Otto, 1885 Novel
Kidnapped, 1886 Novel
The Strange Case of Dr. Jekyll and Mr. Hyde, 1886 Novel
Memoir of Fleeming Jenkin, 1887 Biography
Memories and Portraits, 1887 Essays
The Merry Men and Other Tales, 1887 Stories
The Black Arrow, 1888 Novel
The Master of Ballantrae, 1889 Novel
The Wrong Box (with Lloyd Osbourne), 1889 Novel
In the South Seas, 1890 Travel Book
The Wrecker (with Lloyd Osbourne), 1892 Novel
Catriona, 1893 Novel
Island Nights' Entertainments, 1893 Stories
The Ebb-Tide (with Lloyd Osbourne), 1894 Novel

The Amateur Emigrant, 1895 Travel Book
Records of a Family of Engineers, 1896 Biography
Weir of Hermiston, 1896 Novel
St. Ives, 1897 Novel
Our Samoan Adventure (with Fanny Van de Grift Stevenson), 1956 Travel Book
Cévennes Journal, 1978 Travel Book

Collected Editions

Collected Words of Robert Louis Stevenson. South Seas Edition, 32 vols. New York: Scribners, 1925.

Robert Louis Stevenson: Collected Poems. Ed. Janet Adams Smith. London: Rupert Hart-Davis, 1952.

The Letters of Robert Louis Stevenson. 8 vols. Eds. Bradford A. Booth and Ernest Mehew. New Haven, CT: Yale University Press, 1997.

See also *Selected Letters*. Ed. Ernest Mehew. New Haven, CT: Yale University Press, 1997.

Biography and Criticism

Ambrosini, Richard, and Richard Dury, eds. *Robert Louis Stevenson, Writer of Boundaries*. Madison: University of Wisconsin Press, 2006.

Arata, Stephen. *Fictions of Loss in the Victorian Fin de Siècle*. Cambridge: Cambridge University Press, 1996.

Balfour, Graham. *The Life of Robert Louis Stevenson*. 2 vols. London: Methuen, 1901.

Bell, Ian. *Dreams of Exile: Robert Louis Stevenson: A Biography*. New York: Holt, 1993.

Buckton, Oliver S. *Cruising with Robert Louis Stevenson: Travel, Narrative and the Colonial Body*. Athens: Ohio University Press, 2007.

Calder, Jenni, ed. *Stevenson and Victorian Scotland*. Edinburgh: Edinburgh University Press, 1981.

Daiches, David. *Robert Louis Stevenson and His World*. London: Thames and Hudson, 1973.

Eigner, Edwin M. *Robert Louis Stevenson and the Romantic Tradition*. Princeton, NJ: Princeton University Press, 1966.

Fowler, Alistair. "Parables of Adventure: the Debatable Novels of Robert Louis Stevenson." Pp. 105–29 in Campbell, Ian., ed., *Nineteenth-Century Scottish Fiction*. Manchester, England: Carcanet, 1979.

Furnas, J. C. *Voyages to Windward: The Life of Robert Louis Stevenson*. London: Faber & Faber, 1952.

Gannon, Susan R. "The Illustrator as Interpreter: N. C. Wyeth's Illustrations for the Adventure Novels of Robert Louis Stevenson." *Children's Literature Annual* 19 (1991): Pp. 90–106.

Jones, William B., ed. *Robert Louis Stevenson Reconsidered: New Critical Perspectives*. Jefferson, NC: McFarland, 2003.

Kiely, Robert. *Robert Louis Stevenson and the Fiction of Adventure*. Cambridge, MA: Harvard University Press, 1964.

Lapierre, Alexandra. *A Romance of Destiny: Fanny Stevenson*. Trans. Carol Cosman. New York: Carroll & Graf Publishers, 1995.

Maixner, Paul, ed. *Robert Louis Stevenson: the Critical Heritage*. London: Routledge & Kegan Paul, 1981.

McLynn, Frank. *Robert Louis Stevenson: A Biography*. New York: Random House, 1994.

Mennikoff, Barry. *Narrating Scotland: The Imagination of Robert Louis Stevenson*. Columbia: University of South Carolina Press, 2005.

Nollen, Scott Allen. *Robert Louis Stevenson: Life, Literature, and the Silver Screen*. Jefferson, NC: McFarland, 1994.

Sandison, Alan. *Robert Louis Stevenson and the Appearance of Modernism*. London; Macmillan, 1996.

Showalter, Elaine. *Sexual Anarchy: Gender and Culture at the Fin de Siècle*. New York: Penguin, 1990.

Swearing, Roger G. *The Prose Writing of Robert Louis Stevenson*. Hamden, CT: Archon, 1980.

Veeder, William, and Gordon Hirsch, eds. *Dr. Jekyll and Mr. Hyde After One Hundred Years*. Chicago: University of Chicago Press, 1988.